GOOD ON PAPER

JENNIFER MILLIKIN

JNM, LLC

ISBN-13: 978-1-7326587-2-1
www.jennifermillikinwrites.com

To Luke.
You call yourself analytical, but I think you may be a romantic
after all.

PROLOGUE

TOMORROW I'M GOING TO TELL THAT JACKASS, VINCENT D'Onofrio, that Natalie Maxwell asked me to come to her house to study. I mean, *yeah*, Mrs. Orson made us partners for this project on Ancient Greece. And, *okay*, there's no way she'd have asked me otherwise. Natalie is on the dance team and sits with the cool kids at lunch. She has a lot of dark hair that she tosses around while she laughs with her friends. And then there's me. I exist somewhere in the murky middle. I'm smart, but not enough to be in advanced classes. I'm athletic, but not enough to be on a team. I'm good-looking enough to get dates, but not confident enough to go for a girl like Natalie Maxwell. I'm Aidan Costa, the guy who blends into whatever structure he happens to be walking past.

Until today. In fourth period history, Mrs. Orson announced who our partners are, and my stomach flipped. How could I have gotten so lucky?

After class, Natalie marched up to my desk as I gathered my things and asked me to come over to her house so we can get started on the project. That's right about when I stopped being aware of my own body. Did I even have a stomach anymore? And where did my bones disappear to? I felt like goo held together by skin. Gross, but true.

Now I'm walking through neighborhoods, going in the opposite direction of my house, with Natalie Maxwell by my side. Her forearm has bumped mine twice. *Twice.* I know it's not on purpose, but a guy can dream.

"So," I start, unsure of what to say. Natalie told me it would take ten minutes to walk to her place, and I used up the first four silently begging my underarms to stop sweating. "What's it like to be a preacher's kid?"

Natalie glances at me, then back to the sidewalk. She grips the straps of her backpack in each fist so that her elbows stick out behind her. She tips her head, and the sun hits her at just the right angle to make her hair shimmer. It's almost the exact same shade as mine, but a million times shinier.

"PK," she says, looking back up at me for just a second.

"What?" I ask. I must've heard her wrong.

A smile slips from the side of her mouth at my obvious lack of knowledge. I like this smile. It's different from all her other ones. It's not like I stalk her (I'm not a creep), but it's hard not to notice these things from the bleachers when she and eleven other girls are jumping up and down, pom-poms shaking.

"PK," she repeats. "Preacher's kid."

"Oh. Right." I fall silent, not sure what to say next.

Her smile vanishes and her face looks sad. But not an open kind of sad. More like a hidden sadness, the kind that goes deep down like a well.

"It's not great. People expect more from a preacher's kid.

Do the right thing. Get good grades. Always be nice. Never be anything less than pleasant." She laughs, but the sound is hollow. "Basically, PKs aren't allowed to be human. Sometimes I just want to scream."

"I understand."

"You do?" She stops and looks at me, surprise widening her eyes. I pause too and shove my hands in my pockets.

Natalie must not have heard the rumors. I don't think they can be called rumors, because they're true. I spent a few weeks hiding in the library at lunchtime until things died down.

"My mom writes books. Her first book was a big deal romance novel about her and my dad. It's based on their relationship. Last year some girls found out it was my mom who wrote it and blabbed." I'll never forget the looks on their faces. Like they couldn't believe *my* parents could have a love story like that.

"But aren't you proud of your mom? Unless," Natalie draws out the word as a flush creeps across her cheeks. "Unless it was one of *those* types of books. Like the kind my grandma keeps in her nightstand and thinks nobody knows about." Natalie's lips purse as she waits for my response.

I shake my head. "No no no. Not like that."

Natalie's doing the sort of smile thing again, and the tips of my ears feel hot. To make it more difficult for her to spot my redness, I resume walking. Natalie follows. "It's not the story," I start, wondering how exactly to explain it all. "It's what's happened because of the story. It's a lot of pressure to have parents with a famous romance."

"Like how?"

I wish I could rewind five minutes and go back, then I wouldn't have told Natalie I understood her plight as a PK. I have no desire to explain all this to her, but it's too late for that now. "Girls expect me to be just like them. Or like my dad, I guess. They think I should make the best boyfriend in the world if I come from people like my parents. Flowers, chocolates, twittering birds forming a heart, yada yada."

Natalie's hands wrap around her backpack straps again. "Are you saying you're a bad boyfriend?"

"No." The word rushes from my lips. "I don't really know what I'm saying. Just that I understand, is all."

The hand closest to Natalie, the one dangling between us, suddenly feels warmer than it did a few seconds ago. I look down, watching her fingers snake through mine.

"Thank you," she whispers. I never knew what a grateful smile looked like until this moment. On Natalie, it's closed lip, both sides slightly upturned, and softness in her eyes.

She drops my hand and turns left at the end of the street. I follow her, letting my thoughts fill the quiet that has overtaken us. It's not that I'm a bad boyfriend or a particularly good one. I'm not boyfriend material *at all*. I might have a crush on Natalie, but I would never act on it. She doesn't deserve someone with a secret like the one I'm keeping. It's not the secret that's the problem. It's the fact that I'm keeping it. That I *have* to keep it. How could I be in a relationship and keep a secret this big? By not getting into a relationship in the first place.

"My parents aren't home." Natalie's relieved voice breaks into my thoughts. She stops, scans the street, and walks up to a two-story white house. Is she telling me this for a reason? Does she want to mess around? I may not be boyfriend material, but I'm not opposed to messing around with the girl I've been crushing on for what feels like forever. Not that Natalie would be into me, but I certainly wouldn't turn her down if she lost her mind and decided I'm the lucky guy.

Pulling a key from her backpack, Natalie unlocks the door and opens it. "Come in," she says, beckoning me with a wave of her hand.

She leads me through the living room and into the kitchen. The first thing I notice is how clean the house is. Everything looks like it has been placed there on purpose, not a stray book or tissue in sight.

"Nice house," I tell her, sitting on a stool Natalie has pulled out for me.

"Thanks." She steps into the pantry, pointing above her head as she steps through. I look up and read the words as she recites them. "*This house runs on love and Jesus*. If the sign says it, then it must be true." Sarcasm stains her tone.

Natalie backs out of the pantry holding sandwich cookies, the kind where one side is vanilla and the other chocolate. "These okay?" she asks.

The truth is, I'd eat them even if they were covered in moth dust. My mom never buys cookies like that. She's always on a diet, and the cookies she buys taste like cardboard.

"Uh huh," I nod, fighting the urge to grab them from her hand and eat them Cookie Monster style.

"Let's go out back. It's nice out." Natalie picks up her backpack from the kitchen floor where she dropped it and passes me. Slinging my backpack over my shoulder, I follow her lead to a sliding glass door. Her arms are full, so I reach out and open it for her.

"Leave it open," she tells me. "The house needs some fresh air."

We settle at the table on the patio, both of us tossing our backpacks on top and digging through them for our stuff.

"I brought my laptop," I tell her, sliding the silver computer from my bag.

"Lucky," Natalie says. "We have one computer, and it belongs to the family."

In the next forty-five minutes, I learn two things about Natalie: she's way more creative than me, and her tongue pokes out of the side of her mouth when she's focusing.

"I think we're almost there," Natalie says, tapping the end of her pen against the table.

"We just have to—" I stop short when I hear voices.

"I don't understand why you do that. You knew I was having a luncheon for the staff today. This is the kind of shit you pull."

The voice is coming from inside Natalie's house. I look at her, but she's looking away, her eyes squeezed shut. Her mouth moves, but there is no sound. *Please don't do this right now,* she says, the silent words overflowing with her plea.

"Me?" A second voice, this one screeching. *Natalie's mom?* "I went to the church to bring you lunch. I'm sorry for being a good wife."

"I'm going to go," I tell Natalie, moving to stand. She opens her eyes and looks at me, her expression unfathomable. The voices inside continue, growing louder and more fierce. I shove my stuff in my backpack and hope there's a side gate I can sneak out of. I don't want to walk in on whatever is happening inside Natalie's house.

Our heads turn at the sound of a loud crash, then two slammed doors.

"I'll walk you out," Natalie whispers. Her face is redder than my ears on our walk here.

Pointing inside, I say, "I don't know about going in there right now."

"Don't worry. She's in her bedroom. He's in his office."

So this is normal? It happens often enough that a pattern has developed? I follow Natalie through the house, retracing our steps from an hour ago. We walk back through the living room, only now there is something new about it. The pristine room sports a fist-sized hole in the wall. *Pastor Maxwell has a temper.*

I pause in the door Natalie has held open for me. I can't stand the thought of her staying here in this place. "Come with me," I say, my tone urgent.

"Where?"

"To a place where you can scream."

Natalie casts a look into the house, then back to me. She steps out and closes the door behind her. Taking her hand, I hurry her back down the street, all the way to school, and straight to my car.

She stops when I open the passenger door. "You have a car?"

I nod.

"Why did we walk to my house?" she asks, getting in and looking up at me.

"I don't know," I answer, then close her door. I'm prepared for her to demand a better response, but when I open my door and slide in, she doesn't say anything.

I drive Natalie to a place where she can scream until her throat hurts.

"Hey, Lisa." I wave at the woman behind the desk. "This is Natalie."

Natalie waves and Lisa smiles. She turns back to me. "What do you need, Aidan?"

I make prayer hands and hope I look pathetic enough. "The recording studio for, like, twenty minutes."

Lisa gives me a look. "Come on," I plead.

Lisa sighs but points behind herself with one thumb. "Studio B. Twenty minutes."

Grabbing Natalie's hand, I waste no time getting back there. There are flips and switches everywhere, but we won't need any of those. The room is divided nearly in half by a glass wall and a door. I lead Natalie through the door and into the studio.

"Here," I say, patting the top of a stool the way Natalie did for me in her kitchen earlier. She sits tentatively, looking at me with uncertainty.

"I can't do this," she half-whispers.

"Nobody will hear you."

"Just you."

"I'll leave." Without waiting for her to tell me, I turn around and walk out, closing the door behind me. Glancing back through the glass wall, our eyes meet, and I read her lips. *Thank you.*

I smile tightly and turn around, leaving the room altogether and going to wait in the hallway.

The preacher's daughter is nothing like I thought she would be.

1

NATALIE

Sign it.

Such a simple task. Pick up the pen and sign your name on the line. A few strokes and my name will join his.

Paper bound us, and paper will cement our ending.

Three years ago, on our paper anniversary, Henry handed me a roll of toilet paper. On it, he'd written *I love the shit out of you* in brown Sharpie.

"Mrs. Shay? Do you need a moment?" The attorney we chose has a voice like gravel and kind eyes. That had surprised me. Before him I thought all divorce attorneys were callous, hardened to the emotion spilling out in front of them. My parents' attorneys had dull, lifeless eyes. I assumed years of client theatrics had immunized them to personal anguish.

A deep breath fills my chest, passing slowly through my lips on its way out. I look up into eyes crinkled at the corners. Mr. Rosenstein, our attorney, is dressed in a starched white shirt, navy suit, and plaid bow tie. He may work in New York City, but his outfit says genteel Southerner.

Clearing my throat, I manage to push words past the lump that has formed. "I'm okay. Thank you."

I pick up the pen, its coldness a sharp contrast to my heated palm. My thumb extends, covering the end, and I both hear and feel the click. The sound is thunderous, somehow louder in volume than any of our fights.

How did it come to this?

It's a silly question. I know just how it happened. Epic showdowns decreased in ferocity until the air between us held only silence. Hearts that beat red faded into an unassuming, neutral shade. Eventually we became spectators in the demise of our marriage.

The pen scratches across the paper, my hand making the familiar loops. I dot my *i* and cross my *t*, imagining it as a headline.

Natalie Shay has just signed her divorce papers.

* * *

THIS WAS A MONUMENTALLY BAD IDEA.

I should've said no when Henry suggested it, but of course not. Isn't that one of the reasons I left him? His personality was so big, so overwhelming, so *infiltrating* that I lost my voice. It's hard to stand up and breathe when waves are keeping you down, and that's what Henry became. Wave after wave, big ideas and thoughts and criticisms, rolling over me incessantly. I was choking on my desire to be myself. It was either stay and die, or run. I chose.

Out of habit, or maybe guilt, I agreed to meet him after I

signed the papers. My hand dips into my purse, closing around the small box. I've done that at least a hundred times since I placed it there this morning. For four years I wore the contents of the box on my left hand and I didn't touch it this much.

Henry is late. He's probably mentally preparing for this moment. He'll come in swinging, expecting recrimination of all the ways our divorce is his fault. He's a natural-born arguer. I used to joke that he missed his calling as a litigator. In every joke there is an element of truth, and what I was really saying hid behind the jest. *Please stop arguing with everything I say. Please stop listing the reasons why acupuncture is a sham when I just told you how good it makes me feel. Please stop trying to make me feel small.*

My eyes are on the door when Henry walks in. We've been separated for five months, and still my heart jumps up, settling into my throat. He looks good. Softness settled into his middle a couple years ago, but it's gone now. My departure kick-started a new fitness regimen. Out of boredom? Or is there already someone new? The thought makes me uncomfortable.

Henry scans the small coffeehouse, spots me, and though his eyes light up in recognition, he doesn't smile. He comes my way, saying *excuse me* over and over as he squeezes his large, tall frame through tables of seated people.

When he reaches me, I open my mouth to say hello, but his words are faster. "Did you choose a table at the back just to watch me bump into people?"

His voice is smooth, his volume normal, but his words cut.

I choose to ignore him. There's no use pointing out that I

chose the high-top table so he would be more comfortable. "Hi. How are you?"

He settles onto the stool opposite me and props his elbows on the table. His shirtsleeves are rolled up to reveal muscular forearms. In college, he threw footballs and pretended to bench press me. I was happy and convinced we were meant for one another. Funny how things change.

Henry settles his chin into his cupped hands and gazes at me. "I'm good, Nat. Did you sign?" His expression is neutral, and stupidly I wish there was some emotion there. Where is the anger? Where is the sadness?

"Yep," I say curtly, reaching into my bag. Suddenly I can't wait for this to be over, for him to be gone. "Here." I slide the box across the small space. He takes it, careful not to brush his fingers against mine. Tears swim in my eyes, and I pray they don't spill over. Why am I crying? It's over. It's what I wanted. I initiated it.

My gaze sweeps the room, seeing but not really seeing the long line of people waiting to order. The feel of his stare on my face makes me want to melt into a puddle and seep into the ground.

"Natalie, I—" he pauses, his voice softened by a tinge of regret. "I'm not sure what to say. I don't know how to do this."

"Me neither," I whisper, swiping at my eyes.

"Thanks for giving the ring back to me."

My right hand reaches for my ring finger, rubbing the bare flesh. "It was your grandmother's."

Henry stands, pushing the stool back under the table. "Well, I, uh... I'll see you around. Call me if you need anything." He turns, stops, then shakes his head and laughs disbelievingly. "Never mind. You won't need anything. Aidan is here. Like always."

I lean left and peer around Henry.

Aidan is early. Aidan is always early, but on a day like today, he probably hustled in from Brooklyn after school was finished.

"Shay," Aidan nods at Henry. Calling him Shay is a relic from college.

"Costa." Henry's voice has dropped an octave. He looks back at me, his glare full of meaning, silently hurling his accusations at me, as if they haven't been flung a million times before.

Henry stomps out, bumping into people as he goes.

I look at Aidan. His eyes are on me, his gaze soft. He comes to me, folds my head into his chest, and blocks me from view while I fall apart.

2

AIDAN

NATALIE'S TEXT CAME THROUGH ON MY LUNCH HOUR. I BIT into my sandwich and pulled my phone from my desk.

Natalie: I'm doing it today.

I wrote her back right away. **You're certain?**

Natalie: What's the point of waiting?

I asked her what she needed, and she told me where to meet her. I don't know why Henry wanted to get the ring from her in person, but I wasn't going to say anything. I learned a long time ago not to voice my opinion when it came to Henry.

As soon as the bell rang, I ran to the train. It's a good thing I did, because Natalie needed me. Right now she's curled into me, her hair falling down her back and snot smeared on my blue sweater. She hates crying in public. My back is to the rest of the place, shielding her. The scent of strong coffee and sweet syrup makes my mouth water, but Natalie's not about to let me go. Suppressed sobs shake her shoulders, and I feel the tremble in my chest.

Her heart is breaking. It's been breaking for a long time,

but it's the finality that's getting her now. She didn't imagine this for herself. She wanted forever. Happily ever after wasn't an abstract concept. If I didn't already know this for certain, I'd only have to pick a book off her shelf and read the last twenty pages. The characters in her books always fall in love.

"Nat," I whisper down into her hair. She has a cowlick at the crown, and I learned this years ago, the first time I held her hair while she vomited up strawberry Boone's Farm. "Do you want to go somewhere and get a drink?"

She lifts her chin and looks up at me, swipes a hand under her nose, and nods.

"Let's go."

She grabs her purse and lifts the strap over her head, positioning the bag on her hip.

I pull napkins from the dispenser and hand them to her. "You need to wipe your face."

She smiles and leans over, pretending to wipe her snotty nose on my sleeve. Shoving the napkin into her hand, I keep one and attempt to clean up the front of my sweater.

"Sorry." Natalie frowns apologetically.

"Don't worry. It's not the first time." Turning, I start for the exit. She follows. Amid the noise of conversation, I hear the *tap tap tap* of her heels.

"You threw up on my feet once." Her voice floats into my ears and I cringe. It's not my favorite memory.

"What do I have to do to erase that from your memory?" Pulling the brass door handle, I prop open the door with a foot and let Natalie walk through first.

"I'll never forget it. It was the night you said you loved me." She tucks her hands inside the back pockets of her jeans and peers at me, her head tipped to one side.

"Friend-love," I clarify. I don't do love. Never have. It's better suited for people who are not like me. People like Natalie.

She rolls her eyes. "Well, duh."

"Come on." I start down the crowded sidewalk. Natalie is in step beside me. "I want a beer. The dark kind you can almost chew."

"Gross," Natalie says, wrinkling her nose.

"You know what I mean."

There's a beer garden a few blocks away. We get there, settle into our seats, and Natalie orders a light beer with some kind of fruit in its name.

"So, you're divorced, huh?" I sit back and cross an ankle over the opposite knee.

Natalie scowls.

"I don't know what else to say," I tell her. It's the truth. What does a person say to their best friend right after they've signed their divorce papers?

"I guess so," Natalie says slowly. Even more slowly, she says, "I am divorced. I'm divorced. I'm twenty-eight, and I'm divorced. I married my college sweetheart, and now we're divorced." Her voice is thick by the time she reaches the end of her sentence.

"We don't have to talk about it."

"You don't have anything to say?" Her words are a challenge. I can't blame her. We both know I've never been Henry's biggest fan.

I shake my head and nod my thanks at our server when she sets down our beers.

"Don't go quiet on me now, Costa. I know you have a mouthful of words waiting to tumble out."

"I'm sorry you've had to go through this." Sipping my

beer, I watch her. She surveys me with shrewd eyes, knowing that I'm holding back.

What I want to say is something along the lines of *I knew it would come to this.* Of course I knew. Henry Shay was one of my college roommates. He's not a bad person, and he wasn't back then either. They just weren't right together, no matter how hard Natalie tried. They seemed like they should be right for each other. He played football, she was on the dance team. On every surface, in ways only eyes can see, they looked like a match made in heaven. They fit together. But underneath, geometry doesn't matter. Below the surface is where it gets messy.

Henry was incapable of handling what comes beneath the surface of Natalie. Two years ago, Natalie wrote a book. In the last year, she has sent her manuscript out to at least a hundred different agents. As rejection after rejection rolled in, Natalie became more and more upset. Henry approached Natalie's despondency the only way he knew how: to try and point out what she'd done wrong. What Henry didn't understand was that Natalie had done nothing wrong. When Henry took Natalie to the library to look at books on how to become a better writer, I wrote crude comics on her rejection letters that I knew she'd find later and laugh about. For a while I thought maybe I had the advantage because I knew Natalie a few years longer than Henry, but I stopped thinking that. Henry is so short-sighted, I don't know if he would've ever been able to see Natalie's soul. And yet, despite all this, she loved him.

"You should take this experience and turn it into a book." I'm only half kidding. I bet she could sprinkle some of her talent and magic on it and create a bestseller.

"Yeah, sure." She snorts. "Readers will arrive in droves to learn about my failed marriage."

I shrug. "They might."

"Readers don't want to read a fail. They want a happily ever after. They want a tidy, romantic experience to come in a cute box with the pale pink silk ribbon wrapped around it."

"Why don't you change it up?" I know it's risky suggesting this, given Natalie's current mood, but I forge ahead. "Give them something messy."

Natalie eyes me. "Quit trying to change the subject."

"Did you want to keep talking about your divorce?"

"Not really. Let's talk about you."

"What's there to talk about?"

"How's the new girl?" Natalie raises her eyebrows and puckers her lips.

I run a fingertip over the frost on the outside of my glass. "I'm not sure what you're talking about." Of course I know what she's talking about, there's just no point in discussing the girl I swiped right on recently. She will be like all my other relationships: casual, unimportant, and short in duration.

Natalie sips from her beer but keeps her eyes trained on me. "What's her name?"

"I'm not sure what you're talking about," I repeat.

"You're lying."

"How do you know that?"

"Because your mouth is moving."

I give her a look and she laughs, but her eyes have turned wistful. "My grandpa used to say that."

"I always liked your grandpa." Right before he passed away, Natalie and I went to see him. He placed his frail, liver-spotted hand in my offered hand and asked me if I was going to make an honest woman out of his granddaughter. *She's already engaged*, I wanted to tell him. I only nodded and smiled. I didn't want his last moments to be anything but calm. *He was drugged, he probably thought you were Henry*, Natalie said to me later. She was already nervous about the upcoming wedding, so I didn't tell her that her grandfather had said my name twice and knew exactly who I wasn't.

Rubbing the pad of my middle finger around the top of my glass, I keep going until it makes a tinny, musical sound. "Her name is Allison," I say, keeping my eyes on my makeshift instrument so I don't lose focus and spill.

"Are you seeing her tonight?" Natalie finishes her beer and pushes it to the center of the table.

I stop what I'm doing and look up. The sounds of the bar have replaced the music I was making. Natalie waits for a reply, but I'm trying to read her emotions. Her face is expressionless, but the vulnerability I see in her eyes allows me to read her like a book.

"I'll cancel," I offer, and the second the two words have left my lips she tells me to keep my plans.

"Allison would be very disappointed." Natalie gets the attention of our server and signals for the check.

I grab her hand and pull it down to the table. "We don't have to leave yet. I'm not meeting her until seven."

She slips her hand out from under mine and lightly pinches the top of my hand. "I have to finish packing."

My eyes roll upward, my gaze lifting to the exposed piping in the ceiling. "Shit," I mutter, looking back down to Natalie. "I forgot about that." Weeks ago I'd told her I would help her move.

"It's fine. I don't need help. Honestly," she adds when she sees the look on my face.

I feel like a real asshole. My best friend's moving out of the apartment she shared with her husband and I'm not going to be there to help her.

"Will Savannah come over and help you?" Internally I'm crossing my fingers. Savannah is Natalie's coworker and new roommate.

Natalie opens her mouth but hesitates. Two seconds pass, then she decides to tell me the truth. "Savannah went home to Texas for two weeks. She left yesterday."

That settles it. I'm canceling.

"I'll be fine, Aidan. Really." Natalie gives me her serious look. It's the mom look without being a mom in the first place.

I hold up my hands. "Fine. I believe you." I definitely do not believe her. And there's no way I'm going to let her pack up her apartment alone.

Our server stops by and leaves the check on the table. Natalie reaches for it, but I'm faster. "I got it."

She tries to swipe it from me. "Let me."

"Are you suggesting I can't afford to buy you a beer?"

"You can't."

She's right. Technically, anyway. If I would tap into my trust fund, I could buy every patron in every bar in Manhattan a beer and not put a dent in the pile. But I don't want that money. That money is soaked with years of cover-ups, outright lies, and subject changes. It's not dirty money in the traditional sense, but it might as well be.

"Tonight I can. I got my holiday bonus."

"It's not even Thanksgiving yet."

I lay a twenty on the bill. "Please stop talking."

Natalie laughs. "Never." She points at the bathroom and slides from her seat.

While she's gone, I pull out my phone and send a message to Allison through the dating app. **Something came up. Can I have a raincheck for next Friday night?**

Allison responds immediately, agreeing. Natalie comes back to the table but doesn't sit. She waits for me to swallow the last of my beer and moves aside so I can stand up.

When we get outside, Natalie turns to me. "Thanks for the beer. And for everything else." She steps into me and wraps her arms around my middle. We hug for a moment and she pulls away. "Bye, Aidan." She turns, heading in the direction of her apartment. Or, her soon-to-be old apartment. I follow, making my steps loud on purpose. She turns back and stares at me.

"What are you doing?" Her eyebrows are drawn together in suspicion. She shivers, tucking her hands into her jacket pockets.

"I was thinking about how long it has been since I helped someone move. I'm overdue and I need to check the box before the end of the year. Can you help me out?"

Natalie's head tips to the side. "And Allison?"

Tucking my hands in my own pockets, I shrug and rock back on my heels. "I rescheduled for next Friday night."

In the glow of the streetlight and the traffic, I see the relief filling Natalie's eyes. "Thank you."

Walking forward, I sling an arm around her shoulders and turn her around, steering her down the street.

"Always, Nat."

3

NATALIE

My cereal tastes weird here.

My skin feels drier.

The air smells different. There is still the scent of old wood, the unmistakable layers of tenants past, with one glaring omission: lack of any manly scent. The absence wasn't something I noticed yesterday, not with Aidan here helping me move in, but now it feels like a slap in the face.

A small groan escapes me as I reach into the fridge for the orange juice. My shoulders burn even with that one small movement. I know as the day goes on I will begin to feel the aches in other muscles. So many boxes, so many steps. Thank god I had Aidan.

I pour my juice and turn, studying the front of the fridge. Savannah smiles back at me, her blonde hair and pink tips glowing in the picture's sunlight. She's leaning on an upright snowboard, her free arm wrapped around the waist of her boyfriend, Drew.

The rest of the fridge displays the drawings of Savannah's nieces. Peering closer, I read the childish writing in the corners and learn their names: Zoe and Charlotte.

Like the kitchen, the rest of the apartment is clean and fully stocked. I walk through the place, my free hand running across the back of the couch, then across the top of the table. *Furnished*, Savannah had said when she offered her place to me. *Everything but a bed, but you can buy a new one. You don't have to bring any bad juju furniture with you.* Those words were what I needed to finally sign the papers. Until then I'd been in a fog, stuck in the logistics of it all. When Savannah offered her spare bedroom to me, I finally saw the formation of a plan. Henry took what he wanted to keep, and the rest I sold on Craigslist. Including our bed. Sleeping on my old marriage bed, tangled up in smells and memories? Now *that* would be bad juju.

Aidan was here yesterday when the delivery guys brought in my new bed. Black wrought-iron, the exact type of bed Henry had vetoed when we were picking out our own.

Aidan watched the guys assemble the bed, and when they left, he said, "You know you're going to have to break that in."

I balked. "Excuse me?"

Aidan rolled his eyes. "Not with me. But you know the saying. The best way to get over someone is to get under someone else."

I let the comment pass. Now, looking at my bed in the bright morning light, I wonder if he's on to something. The idea repulses and intrigues me in equal amounts. I'm not surprised Aidan suggested it. Casual sex is the only kind of sex he has. I've never understood why he's against relationships. Of all people, he's the poster boy for falling in love.

Twenty years ago his mom wrote a book about her romance with his dad, and it still resonates in the hearts and minds of readers everywhere. My own mother read and re-read the book until the binding was bent and lined. When I was older, I bought my own new copy and fell in love with the idea of love. Not just any love though. Nothing like the love my parents had, if that could even be called love. I wanted what Aidan's parents had. Blinding, sweeping, lose all reasoning love.

Setting my juice glass on the dresser, I look around and survey the scene. Boxes cover a majority of the wood floor, some stacked four high. I walk over to the ones marked *CLOSET*, courtesy of Aidan, and open the top box. I unpack until my cell phone rings from its spot next to my forgotten juice.

Reaching, I grab for the phone and see my sister's name flashing across the screen.

"Hey, Sydney." Two sweaters fall from my hands as I juggle the phone and get it tucked securely between my left ear and shoulder. "Everything okay?"

"That's what I should be asking you. I'm calling to see how Friday went. Signing the papers." Her curious tone changes to dread. "You did sign them, didn't you?"

"Yes," I respond, trying to keep the irritation I'm feeling from slipping out. Bending, I snatch the two fallen sweaters from the floor and refold them, adding them to the stack on my bed.

"Don't be mad," Sydney says, seeing right through me. "You were waffling."

"You'll understand how it feels when you're preparing to sign your divorce papers. Whenever that may be." *Shit.*

That's not what I meant to say. My eyes squeeze together as I wait for her response.

"Probably never. I'll be in school until I'm old and gray. I'm already getting wrinkles. All the late nights." She yawns as if the mention of late nights has reminded her that she's tired.

"You're no good unless you're sleeping well." My voice has turned gentle but authoritative, motherly.

Sydney yawns again. "Let me know when you invent a twenty-seven hour day, and then we'll talk. Until then, this future Juris Doctor must keep her nose in a book."

Sydney is five years younger than me but light years more intelligent. Growing up, she scoffed at my romance novels and rejected any notion of Prince Charming. Four years of college and one bachelor's degree was enough for me, but not Sydney. She double-majored in Business and Accounting, then went on to Georgetown Law. She's in her second year and every time I talk to her, she sounds like she's on the verge of a mental breakdown. Two years ago, when my marriage was beginning to feel more bad than good, I'd envied Sydney's ambition and freedom of choice. Eventually I realized I had a choice too, even though it was one I never wanted to make. Sydney entered into a relationship with law school, her passion and dedication to the subject nearly as binding.

"Do you want to take a break from studying? FaceTime date?" Ten bucks says my sister has her hair piled crazily on the top of her head.

"I'm taking a break from studying by calling you."

"FaceTime me and I'll show you my new place."

"K bye." She hangs up and four seconds later my phone rings again. I hit the button and the video comes on.

"Hi." I wave. She waves back, then tightens the bird's nest of hair piled on her head. My heart swells at the sight of her. Bags droop beneath her eyes, and her shoulders are hunched even though she's not currently pouring over a textbook. *My baby sister.*

She sniffs and reaches for something off-screen, popping what I think is a potato chip into her mouth. "Show me your digs."

I take her on the tour and she oohs and ahhs at the brick walls and shabby, chipped paint columns in the middle of the place. "Very industrial, post-modern New York." She nods and applauds.

I laugh. "Do you even know what you're talking about?"

"Nope," she says, popping the 'p.' "Is Savannah there? Did she help you move in?"

I shake my head, and at the same time say, "Aidan."

"Ah, yes. Of course. I'm sure that pleased Henry."

"Henry wasn't there when I moved. He's staying with a friend, remember?"

"I know, but I was imagining he'd be there to say goodbye or something."

My eyebrows pull tight. "Do you remember Henry?"

Sydney laughs. "My fault. I've been watching snippets of Hallmark movies when I need to clear my head."

"Watch it," I say, wagging a finger at the screen. "Next you might accidentally read a romance novel."

She scoffs. "The first romance novel I read will be yours. And the second one will be your second novel." She waves an arm. "And so on and so on."

"These days I hardly feel like writing."

"You will soon. You're too good not to."

"You've never even read anything I've written."

Her bun flops over wildly as she shakes her head. "Not true. You write a mean grocery list."

I nod. "I am good at grocery lists."

Sydney laughs and an immense wave of sadness sweeps me. I'm alone on a Sunday. No roommate, no husband. No family. Just a life in boxes.

"Where'd you go?" Sydney asks. "I can see you, but I get the feeling you're no longer there."

"Still here," I sniffle.

"I'm loving you from DC, okay?"

I nod. "I'm loving you from NYC."

Sydney shifts, and behind her, I see an unmade bed and clothes everywhere. "Will you promise me something?"

I nod.

"Call me if you get sad. Or call Aidan. Don't call Mom though. She'd just bash your whole marriage."

I laugh softly. "You got it."

"Bye, babe." She blows me a kiss.

"See ya, toots." I return her kiss and press the end button.

Tucking my phone into my pocket, I walk back to my room and keep unpacking. When I'm finished with my closet and my dresser drawers are full, I take a shower and blow dry my hair. I gather a hairbrush, two types of combs, hairspray, hair clips, and small plastic rubber bands. Armed with all these things, I plant myself in front of my computer and pull up YouTube. Navigating to my favorite channel, I choose a video and watch the young woman demonstrate a complicated braid. For the next hour, I start and stop the video, following along, until I've braided my hair like hers. I messed up four times and had to restart, but I did it.

4

AIDAN

"You know, Mrs. Jones, you and I would make a dashing couple." Grinning at Mrs. Jones, I poke through the candy bowl she keeps on the end of her desk. I'm after the Milky Way I spied near the bottom of the bowl, but the gluttony of Snickers keeps getting in my way. This is probably because I've been in here every day this week, picking my favorites until I'm left with second best.

Mrs. Jones laughs, and it makes my smile grow. Her laugh is unique, to put it mildly. It's more like a hoot, because it literally sounds like she's saying "hoo" with each breath. "You'd have to fight my husband," she responds, placing a flattened palm on the desk and pushing herself to standing.

She wobbles, and I hurry around the desk to help, but she shoos me away.

"Doesn't let this skin suit fool you, Mr. Costa. I'm spry on the inside."

She walks slowly to the copy machine and pushes a button while I make a second pass through her candy bowl.

The machine whirs to life, making its high pitched sounds, and Mrs. Jones turns back to me.

"I know you just pocketed another candy bar, Mr. Costa."

My fingers tighten around the candy in my pocket. "They're fun size," I argue. "Who can eat only one?"

Mrs. Jones makes a *tsk* sound and turns back to the copier.

When I get back to my classroom, I pop the second candy bar into my mouth. Lunch will be over soon, and my classroom will fill with loud, well-meaning, mostly obnoxious sixteen and seventeen-year-olds. For now, I'm enjoying the final few minutes of peace.

Sitting down at my desk, I pull out my phone and see a message from Natalie.

I need a boozy lunch.

What? Since when does 'little miss *day drinking doesn't agree with me*' need a boozy lunch?

I was with her on the day she made that rule for herself. I remember precisely why, too. She day drank, passed out at three in the afternoon, and I broke the lock on her dorm room door trying to get to her because I was worried she had alcohol poisoning. I was plastered too, and it didn't occur to me to find her roommate to unlock the door.

What's going on? I ask, but she doesn't respond immediately. Every day since last Saturday when I helped Natalie move into her new place, I've texted her asking how she's doing. She responds with one word: *good.* I know next to nothing about females, but I'm an expert in Natalie, and I knew she needed space.

My last precious minute of teenager-free time is spent staring at the phone, waiting for the three little dots to appear. The bell rings and they pour in without any word from Natalie. I stow my phone in the top drawer of my desk and watch the kids trickle in. I smile and nod as they slide into their seats. Some faces are bored, some are sullen, and one person has his hat over his face and his head tipped back. Per usual, I'm missing one student in particular. When the last bell rings, I rise from my seat and stick my head out the door. Sure enough, Adam Harris and his girlfriend, Linzie something, are making out like only horny teenagers can.

"Mr. Harris, on your own time please." My voice is gruff because I'm an authority figure, but my seventeen-year-old self is cheering him on.

Linzie giggles and extricates herself from Adam, hurrying away. Adam saunters over with enough swagger for the both of us.

"Sorry, Mr. C."

No, you're not. You heard the bell. Can't blame the kid though.

"No problem." I reach out, patting his back as he passes me. "You get first turn at the board. Trigonometry waits for no man."

He groans audibly and a few people laugh as he tosses his bag on his desk. While Adam's at the board, I pull open my desk drawer and act like I'm looking for something, but I'm checking my phone. Nothing from Natalie. I really hope she's not day drinking on her own. Who the hell knows what will happen.

* * *

"NATALIE, OPEN UP." I KNOCK AGAIN, HARDER THIS TIME. I know she's in there. The second my feet hit the landing I could hear the sounds of a cheesy romance movie filtering under her door. When the rest of the day passed and I still didn't hear back from her, I decided an in-person check was in order.

The door swings open. Natalie's puffy, red eyes meet mine.

"What's wrong?" Hurrying in, I grab her hand from the door handle and pull her into me. Her head collapses into my chest, her scent wafting up to my nose. Natalie always smells the same, but I've never been able to describe it. It's just her smell. My Nat.

"He chose the other woman," she sobs. "He proposed."

My lips press together, my eyebrows scrunch. "Nat," I say, and she pulls back. Tears stick to her eyelashes. She blinks, freeing a few of them and sending them cascading down her face. "Who are you talking about?"

Pressing her face back against my shirt, she mumbles, "Movie."

It's hard work, but I keep my chest from moving as my silent laughter tumbles through me. Getting teary-eyed over a movie? It's so Natalie. Still, my best friend alarm is in tip-top condition, and its alarm bells are going off right now. Natalie might get teary-eyed over nearly everything, but she doesn't *sob*.

"What else?" I ask.

She pulls back again, and this time all her tears have either dried or transferred to the front of my shirt. When she hesitates, I urge her on by saying, "Out with it."

My arms drop to my sides when she turns abruptly. She

walks back to the couch, pushes aside the oversized blanket crumpled on top, and mutes the TV.

Following her lead, I cross her new apartment and sit down. This is only my second time in this place and I'm already more comfortable here than I was at her old place. Henry played nice on the surface, but there was always an edge to his words, an unwelcoming energy emanating from him. I got the feeling he put up with me for Natalie's sake. Even when we lived together in college, it was because I needed a place to live and Natalie asked if I could take his open room.

Nat's new place is nice. Exposed brick walls, black and white art hung from rustic nails, an herb garden next to the window with the best light. Even with a roommate to split the rent, Natalie is doing well for herself. Settling for that accounting job paid off for her. Monetarily speaking, anyway. Me, on the other hand... well, I'm a teacher. I live with two other dudes and we all share a bathroom. Those are the breaks when you live in New York City. Sometimes I brush my teeth in the kitchen because one of my roommates is in the bathroom, but if I want, I can have Chinese delivered at three a.m. Gotta take the good with the bad.

Natalie folds her legs into her body, tucking them up into the oversized gray sweatshirt she's wearing. Her knees nearly poke out the neck hole, and she rests her chin on the space between them. Her eyes fall to a piece of paper on the coffee table.

"I had my mail forwarded, but it's not effective yet. On my lunch break, I went to pick up mail from my old place. Now I wish I hadn't." Her voice is tiny, despair poking through the space between her words. "Another rejection letter."

Shit. This isn't like all the other rejection letters. This is from the agent who requested Natalie's manuscript. This rejection carries more weight, and at the worst time. Leaning forward, I capture the paper from the coffee table with two fingers and start to read.

DEAR MS. SHAY,

Your writing style is lovely. You are very talented. I am rejecting Much Ado About You because it's too sweet. Readers want to feel desire when reading romance, and while your book had a great romantic element, there wasn't enough sexual tension, or realized sex, to keep readers of this genre turning the pages.

Thank you,
Christina Evans

TO ME, THIS DOES NOT SOUND LIKE A PROBLEM. READERS want sex? Write sex. End of discussion.

But I know better than to say that.

"Hmm," I say instead, setting the letter next to me on the couch.

Natalie narrows her eyes. "Don't say it."

"I didn't say anything." I lean back against a pillow and cross an ankle over the opposite knee.

"Your face is saying it for you."

"I can't control what my face does."

"Actually, you can."

Scrunching up my eyes, I bare my teeth and attempt to push my lips in opposite directions.

Natalie laughs. "Ew. Stop that right now. It looks awful."

My lips burn as they return to normal, but I made Natalie laugh. Mission accomplished.

"Are you going to write more sex?"

"I don't want to." She bites her lower lip, looking away. Following her eyes to the TV screen, I see what she sees: a man on bent knee in the pouring rain, while a woman cries and holds her hands to her mouth. It makes me cringe. When I look back at Natalie, she's got this yearning look in her eyes.

She points at the screen. "I write that. I take characters and I make them feel real."

"Real people have sex." This is needless to point out, but Natalie needs a good kick in the direction of reality. She's so bogged down by the fairy tale that she misses reality.

Natalie looks back to me. "I'm aware of that. But the kind of sex they want me to write has a lot of words that feel unauthentic to me."

My interest is officially piqued. "How do you know that?"

"Before I went back to work today, I looked through the romance category on Amazon. I bought a couple of books and skimmed them and"—Natalie points at the paper beside me—"the agent is right. My heat level is nothing like them."

"What kind of words do they use?" I can't help my smirk. This should be fun.

She grabs the remote from the arm of the couch and lifts it. I know what she's going to do, and I pluck it from her hands before she can hit play.

"Just say it, Nat. You won't burst into flames. Nobody is here but us."

Burying her head in the crook of an elbow, she says, "Plunge. Drive. Writhe. Flick. And so many more."

"You know, a car can *plunge* over a guard rail. A person can *writhe* in pain."

She removes her arm and lifts her head. "Not in this context."

I smile. I can't help it. "You need to loosen up."

"I'm loose," she argues.

I give her a look. She grins sheepishly. "Wrong context?" I ask.

She nods and pulls her legs out from under her sweatshirt. "I don't want to write steamy sex. It's as simple as that."

"Do you want to *have* steamy sex?"

She ignores me. "How was school today?"

"C'mon, Natalie. It's not going to kill you to talk about it."

"I am not discussing my sex life with you."

"Why? I'm your best friend. I thought women tell their best friend's all the dirty details."

"I think that rule changes if the best friend is a heterosexual of the opposite gender."

"Stupid rule," I say, backhanding the air between us.

Natalie shrugs. I can tell she's digging in her heels.

"School was fine," I answer, lifting my arms and intertwining my fingers around the back of my head. "Same as usual."

"Did you flirt with the old lady again?" Natalie grins.

"Of course," I say. "I've been doing it for so long I think it would hurt her feelings if I stop."

"You know," Natalie says, her pointer finger tracing the lines in a couch cushion. "I added that to my manuscript after you read it. I can't remember if I told you."

"You had the hero flirt with an old lady?"

She nods. "It showed the reader a side of him that was

hidden. He didn't flirt in an obnoxious way. In a sweet, kind way."

A weird part of me feels honored. If she put my actions in a book, it means she thinks highly of me. In this one way, at least. She's made no secret her distaste of my dating choices. If you could call what I do 'dating.' Essentially, it goes something like this: show up at a previously agreed upon spot, make small talk, decipher if the other person is a serial killer who wants to hang us up on a meat hook and make tiny cuts all over our body, and then decide if we want it to turn into sex. End of story.

Natalie tips her head to the side. "Isn't tonight your date thing? Can you call it a date if you're only meeting for sex?" She glances into her kitchen as she speaks. She's probably mentally sifting through her fridge for dinner options.

My silence answers for me. Natalie's eyes take on a knowing look, and then she rolls them.

"Allison, right?" she asks.

I nod reluctantly. I really hate talking about this with Natalie.

"Any chance she could be the one?"

I make a face and Natalie laughs.

Despite our differences, we're careful not to judge one another too harshly, or too openly. She wants Prince Charming on a white horse, I don't believe in love at all. In a nutshell, this is why we work.

"Brunch tomorrow?" I ask her.

She nods, leans back on a pillow, and stretches out, tucking her toes under my thigh.

I know the answer to the question before I ask it, but it's worth a shot. "Do you want me to pass your manuscript to my mom?"

"No, but thank you." I feel her toes wiggling under my thigh. "I want to make it because I'm good enough, not because I have an in."

Grabbing the remote, she turns the movie back on.

This is what we do for the next hour before my date with Allison, where I will meet her at the bar for a drink, and presumably go back to my place and do the things Natalie refuses to write about. I watch a sappy, unrealistic movie about love.

Why do I do this when I firmly do not believe in the institution?

Because.

Because I'll do anything for Natalie.

5

NATALIE

Nine o'clock is a normal time to show up at someone's front door and demand brunch, right? Because that's what I'm about to do.

Hopefully Aidan's date is long gone. Honestly, I don't know how he does it, especially with those roommates of his. Who wants to get busy when there are so many people around?

Lifting my hand, I knock my signature knock, the one all three guys tease me about. The first time they teased me, I felt embarrassed. Every time thereafter, I felt included, like I'd been let into a secret club. If they disliked me, they wouldn't look my way twice. It's kind of like that dumbass rule from the elementary school playground— if they hit you, it means they like you.

Rob answers the door, his shaggy blonde hair falling into his eyes. "You need your own key, Best. I was sleeping."

I shrug at his complaint, but inside I'm grinning. I love my nickname. At first, I thought it stood for best friend, but

Rob explained it's because I'm the best girl Aidan has ever brought into this apartment.

"Does he have company?" I whisper, walking farther in and lowering my purse onto the table that doubles as a desk.

"He did last night. I'm not sure if she's still here." He points to himself. "Asleep, remember?" Rob walks into the kitchen, feet dragging on the wood floor, and grabs a box of cereal from on top of the fridge. "You want?" he holds the box out.

Shaking my head, I tell him I'm supposed to be having brunch with Aidan.

Rob looks at the time on the microwave. "Kind of early," he says, then shoves a massive bite of cereal into his mouth.

I squint at the utensil in his hand. "Is that a serving spoon?"

He glances at it on its way up to his mouth. "Guess so. I'm not sure what a serving spoon looks like."

My lips twist with contained laughter. Rob settles into a seat next to my purse, pushing it aside and motioning to the empty seat across from him. Ignoring the grumble in my stomach, I sink down into the mismatched chair.

"Where's Aaron?"

"Sleeping. How's life?" Rob asks, not knowing he's asking the very question I do not want to answer. *I'm a divorcee who writes saccharin romances and gets rejected more than the last item at the bottom of a discount bin.*

"Fine," I chirp, my tone false, but I know Rob won't catch it. "How is your mom?"

Rob's dad blindsided his mom with divorce papers last summer. Since then she chopped and dyed her hair, lost twenty pounds, and found herself a man she refers to as

Croatian Sensation. Rob is generally disgusted by it all, but I think he's secretly happy for his mom.

"She called a couple days ago from Maui." He pauses to roll his eyes. "She hiked a mountain and it was *life-changing*." Another eye roll *and* a head shake.

"That's good, maybe—"

A door opens. Hushed voices.

I look to Rob, but he's looking down into his cereal bowl, intent on capturing the final bits of Cinnamon Toast Crunch.

Footsteps. One set a soft thud, the other a slap against the wood floor. *Last night's heels.*

I sneak a glance down the hall. Aidan and the mystery woman appear. She looks sleepy, but her makeup is still mostly in place. No mascara streaking. She does morning-after well. Rob and I are quiet as they pass us, and then Rob kicks me lightly under the table.

"JBF hair," he whispers.

I look just in time to see the small rat's nest at the back of her head. She steps out and Aidan follows her into the hall. He's back inside in less than ten seconds. I'm just guessing here, but that probably wasn't the goodbye she had envisioned.

"You're here early." Aidan sinks into a seat beside me. He reaches out, running a hand over my brown wavy hair and messing it up on purpose.

I bat his hand away and ask if he's washed his hands recently. Instead of answering, he rolls his eyes.

"I want brunch," I say, shifting in my seat so I can look at him. The corners of his eyes are red, and in the left one, a little bit of sleep is crusted in the corner. His hair, nearly the same shade as mine, is rumpled.

Aidan yawns, nodding at the same time. "Where?"

I give him a look.

His eyes widen and it's probably the first time since he woke up they've been so open. "Really?"

I nod. I want grease. I want sugar. I want the things I never allow myself to have. The ultra healthy diet I adopted after college is not invited to brunch.

Worry cinches Aidan's eyebrows. "Should I be happy or terrified?"

"Neither," I say, trying to tune out the sound of Rob slurping milk from his bowl. "I'm not sick. Nobody died."

Relief settles onto Aidan's face, pushing his eyebrows to their normal spot. "Give me ten minutes to shower and we'll go." He knocks on the table with two knuckles and stands.

Rob goes to the couch and turns on the TV while Aidan showers. I check my email and daydream about red velvet pancakes. And bacon. And a spicy Bloody Mary.

* * *

"THANK YOU," AIDAN TELLS OUR SERVER, SMILING AT HER. Flustered, she backs into another server, nearly upsetting his tray. Her cheeks pink and she hurries away.

"Way to go," I say, pulling the celery stalk from my drink and taking a loud bite. "I hope she doesn't forget our order now."

Aidan shrugs. "Can't help it. I didn't ask her to get twitterpated."

"Twitterpated? Seriously?"

"Technical term. As a writer, you really should already know that." Aidan removes everything from his Bloody Mary, including the straw, and lays it out on a napkin.

"Unnecessary," he explains, motioning at the discarded vegetables before taking a drink.

I don't agree. I leave everything in.

"So," he says, setting the drink down and pushing it away. "Are you going to tell me you stayed up all night writing hot sex scenes?"

Heat creeps through me at the thought.

Aidan sits back against his side of the booth, his lips twitching with the laughter he's keeping contained. "Come on. Confess."

"You know I didn't." I grab my own drink and take a long pull through the straw. The heat of it makes me cough, and I reach for my ice water, thankful I thought to ask our twitter-pated server for a glass of water alongside my drink.

Aidan watches me, his thumb running across his bottom lip. "Don't you think it might be time you got over that?"

"Says the guy who had meaningless sex last night."

He shakes his head. "Says the guy who had meaningless sex last night *and* this morning."

I feign shock. "A two-fer?"

Aidan's shoulders shake as he laughs. When his laughter subsides, he grows serious. "I think I've figured it out. You wrote a book for two people who don't love each other. And no matter how many happy endings you write, they will never have one."

Ouch. Aidan always knows how to get to the heart of a matter. If there were an arrow lodged in a tree trunk, Aidan's words could be the arrow to split the existing arrow in half. His words are simple and honest. Painful to hear, and his accuracy even more painful to admit.

He continues. "If you weren't writing for them, what kind of book would you write?"

I don't respond, mostly because I'm not sure what to say. I grab hold of my straw and make designs on the surface of my drink. The red liquid dips and sways, little flecks of black pepper disappearing and floating back up to the surface.

What kind of book would I write if I didn't write the happily ever after my parents never had? I...don't know. I love romance. The angst, the desire, the tension, and at the bottom of it all, the one feeling that connects us all. *Love*. We all want it, we all need it. Love ignites passion and causes wars. It instills fear in the bravest of us, and the threat of its removal brings the strongest to their knees.

I want it for myself as much as I wanted it for my parents.

My parents tried. They were in love when I was a little kid, I'm positive of that. Something happened. What I saw were small hurts that led to pain-soaked side comments and passive-aggressive arguments. Then came the aggressive arguments, the holes in the walls, the bruises on my mom's arms from where he'd grab her while they argued. And then, what I now understand to be the silent marriage killer: Indifference. At the time, I didn't know what it meant when my dad had to work late, and my mom didn't appear to care. I was just relieved they were no longer fighting. What I didn't understand was that it meant neither believed there was anything to fight for.

My room became my refuge, and I put my nose in a book and came out only when necessary. Romantic novels were my escape, and I pictured my parents as the heroine and hero. Until the steamy scenes, anyhow.

Flash forward ten years, and I'm operating as the adult version of that girl. Adult me is divorced, lives in New York City, makes a living at a soul-sucking job, and receives rejection letters at an impressive rate. How can I tell my teenage self that this is what she will become?

I look up at Aidan, and my heart floods with how grateful I am for him. His eyebrows lift, and I realize he's still waiting on my answer.

"I don't know. Romance, definitely. I love love. It's a sickness for which there is no cure."

"You still wouldn't let your characters get it on even if you weren't picturing your mom and dad while writing?" Aidan raises his eyebrows.

"My characters get it on," I reply, just as the server drops off our breakfast. It's probably not the weirdest sentence she's ever heard at one of her tables.

Aidan thanks the server and picks up his fork. He stabs the air between us before using it to pick up a link of turkey sausage. "Your characters do not get it on. They have chaste kisses." He takes a bite, chews, and continues. "Side note, that's the first time I've ever used the word chaste."

"God knows you've never behaved that way." I cut off a piece of my pancake and take a bite. *Yum.* Warm. Fluffy. Sweet icing. *Eat those feelings, Natalie.* Normally I'm a 'clean eater' as my sister puts it. Vegetables all day, no carbs after four in the afternoon, lean protein, blah blah blah. But when I'm sad, I eat. If I told Sydney, she'd tell me to find a better way to handle my feelings. Precisely why I don't tell my sister.

"Is that what you wanted?" Aidan nods at my next forkful.

"Um hmmm," I answer, chewing.

"Why do you write chaste kisses, Natalie?"

I stare at him, confused. He knows my reason. Why ask me?

"Childhood trauma can only be your excuse for so long. Why else do you write the way you do?" He leans forward, forearms pressing into the edge of the table. For someone who's asking a question, he doesn't have the look of someone with a query. His eyes are warm. Confident. Knowing.

"Just say it," I tell him. "You obviously think you have a direct line to my brain."

He laughs. "In college I majored in What Natalie Isn't Saying."

I laugh too. I can't help it. "Well, come on then," I say, motioning with one hand. "Lay it on me." Picking up a slice of thick-cut bacon, I munch and wait for Aidan to answer.

He eyes me for a second, places his palms on the table, and pushes to stand. He steps away from his side of the booth, only to slide into mine. His leg bumps mine, and I slide down, making room for him. "What are you doing?"

He still doesn't answer. Using two fingers, he pulls the bacon from my own two fingers and tosses it on my plate.

"Aid—" The rest of his name is stolen from my mouth. The tip of his pointer finger is on top of my right hand and he's sliding it up my bare arm, past my elbow, up to my shoulder.

I'm too shocked to speak, too shocked to move, too shocked to even breathe.

His finger continues across my collarbone, tickling up my neck and to the far corner of my jaw, where his one finger multiplies into all five. He turns my head so I'm facing him, and I look into his eyes, searching for an explanation. In all our years of friendship, he has never touched me this way. When I get to his eyes, I find his gaze not on my own, but on my lips. He sucks his lower lip into his mouth and lets it slide back out.

I start to ask a question, but then he leans in, pressing his lips to the space beside my ear. "In a book, whatever followed me touching you like this, would not be chaste."

At once every part of him that's touching me disappears. He leaves my side of the booth and sits back down. He takes a bite of eggs and looks up at me like nothing happened.

"You're flushed." He points at my face with his fork.

"No shit," I mutter, looking for something to throw at him. Aside from my cutlery, there is nothing I can throw that would do only minor damage. "I was attacked by a one-fingered bandit." Retrieving my bacon, I stuff the rest of it in my mouth and glare at him. "Why the hell did you do that?"

"Material," he says. "Now you can go home and write about the kind of kiss that would come after a lead-in like that."

"Pretty sure of yourself, aren't you?"

"Your cheeks tell me my effort was not in vain."

Cupping my hands, I place them on my traitorous cheeks and give him a dirty look. "Extreme surprise causes flushing too."

Aidan's eyes grow wide. "That's it," he says, his hand shaking with excitement. A forkful of eggs tumbles to his plate.

"What?" I'm still not over what he just did to me. I'm not sure if I should be angry. I don't feel angry, but it seems to be the right emotion to have when your best friend does what he just did.

"Are you free tonight?" he asks, then chuckles. "Why do I even ask? Of course you're free. I'm coming over to—"

"I have plans, actually." I cross my arms. Now I'm mad.

Aidan waves off my plans without hearing them. "Old movies at that crappy little theater don't count."

"They do too." I love those movies. Tonight they're playing *Gone With the Wind*, and I want to watch it. I haven't read the book since high school.

"Cancel that plan. I'm coming over and we're setting up an online dating profile."

"Nope." I shake my head. "No in every language, in every way a person can say it. No."

Aidan crosses his arms and looks at me. "I'll see the movie with you tonight."

I twist my lips and look away. Behind the bar, a guy in a white T-shirt throws a towel over one shoulder and presses buttons on a gigantic, complicated looking coffee machine. The Bloody Mary has settled into my veins, the vodka covering me in a soft, gauzy haze. I should probably order a coffee soon.

I look back to Aidan. Excitement lights up his eyes. He senses I'm about to cave. For years I've tried to get him to watch old movies with me, and for years he has refused. *Sappy romances are my limit.* I can practically hear him saying it.

Creating an online dating profile doesn't mean I'll actually have to *use* it. It can collect dust in the farthest corner of the internet.

I reach my hand across the table. "Deal?"

Aidan places his warm hand in my own and grins. "Deal."

6

AIDAN

Natalie is probably going to kill me. And by probably, I mean definitely.

Her face is looking at me right now, eyes peering at me from behind my computer screen. Her eyes are unique. A blend of blue and green. *Sea green*, she once called it. Her lips lift up on one side, a typical Natalie smirk. She always looks at me that way. It's a mix of exasperation and indulgence. I drive her nuts, but she can't help but love me.

I'm not doing this because I think I know what's best for Natalie. She may think that, but it's not true. I don't know what's best for her. I don't know what she needs right now as she navigates life post-divorce. Does she need a swift kick in the ass or a gentle hug? I suppose me setting up a profile for her falls somewhere in the middle, perhaps an assertive shoulder shove in the right direction. Maybe I do think I know what's best for her.

Leaning back in my chair, I cradle the back of my head in two hands and look at the picture I chose. I had a picture with her full, toothy smile, but I chose the smirk. She's seated on a park bench, her long dark hair spilling over one shoulder. I took the picture last fall. We'd agreed to meet at four, and I would've been on time, but a student caught me after last period and asked for help with the homework I'd assigned. Natalie was sitting there waiting for me. She turned and saw me, so I took out my phone and pretended to film her.

"A rare spotting, folks." I approached cautiously, head bent, and spoke in an accent that toed an obscure line between Australian and English. "This is the wild Natalia Animalus, so named for her thick mane and dedication to punctuality." She laughed, and it spurred me on. I crept closer in exaggerated caution. "The Natalia is a solitary creature, preferring to live and hunt alone. In her head, she concocts stories about others of her kind."

Natalie sat back against the bench, her legs crossed at the ankle, and smirked. That's when I took the picture.

The guys who see this photo will never know the story behind it. A smirk meant for me will mean nothing to them. For a second, I consider taking it down and using the other one. Maybe this one is too special. A moment between best friends captured off-handedly.

The front door of my apartment opens, and Rob and Aaron walk in. Rob throws his jacket on the table, sending a half-dozen droplets of water flying onto my computer screen. I use the bottom of my T-shirt to wipe them off, then shut the computer and lay it on the table.

"Still raining?" I ask, even though it's obvious the storm hasn't let up.

Rob's walking into the kitchen, his back to me, but asks, "Why was a picture of Natalie on your computer?" He pauses, whips around with eyes wide, and says, "Were you... you know... to Best?"

"No," I say loudly, making a face. "Fuck, Rob, are you serious?"

Relief relaxes his eyebrows and brings his eyes back to normal size. "Good. Can't have you getting a crush. Opposite sex friendships are like a delicate ecosystem. One wrong move somewhere in the food chain and the whole thing implodes."

Aaron rolls his eyes and shakes his head. He's a quiet guy, which is a godsend in a small apartment where one of the inhabitants is a guy like Rob. Physically, Rob does not take up a lot of space. But his energy, his presence, his personality, sometimes fill the space like an infinitely expandable balloon.

I grab my glass of water and laptop off the table. "Next time I want your two cents, I'll hand you two pennies."

Rob laughs and opens a bag of chips. "I'm just making sure you know the rules, Aidan." He walks the few feet from the kitchen to the table and tosses down the bag.

Tucking the computer between my arm and my chest, I reach in and take a handful. "I didn't know there were rules."

Rob crunches a chip and gives me a derisive look. "Of course there are rules. Don't you think one of us" —he gestures between himself and Aaron— "would've asked Natalie out by now if there weren't rules?"

I get what he's saying, but just to fuck with him, I act like I don't. "Ask her out. I don't care." False. I do care. Natalie wants the world, and neither of these guys are equipped to give it to her. It would end with one-sided heartbreak and a best friend who wouldn't come to my door ever again.

Rob and Aaron both shake their heads.

"We like Natalie," Rob says, and Aaron shakes his head again. "Therefore, we do not date Natalie. She's undateable. Off-limits. Just like she is to you, apparently."

"Great, good to know we're all on the same page." I stuff three chips in my mouth, then wish I had somewhere to spit them. I force them down and drink most of my water. "Those are disgusting."

"Buffalo bleu cheese." Rob licks chip dust off two of his fingers. "So, why were you looking at a picture of her on your computer?"

"Natalie can tell you if she wants." It's her business, not theirs, and something tells me Natalie doesn't want her online dating profile to become a hot topic with my room-mates. Turning, I make my way to my bedroom. There are only two, but I get my own because I pay half the rent. Aaron and Rob split the second half of the rent because they share the second bedroom, using a curtain to divide the room and give them privacy.

Someone must've turned on the TV, because as soon as I shut the door, I hear the sounds of a baseball game. Lying back on my unmade bed, I open the computer. Natalie's face stares back at me, but in my head, I hear Rob's question. *"Were you... you know... to Best?"*

My stomach feels a little sick. It's either the disgusting chips or the thought of doing *that* to Natalie's image.

Quickly I shut the computer and push it off to the side. I get up, go out to the kitchen, and grab a beer. There are two hours to kill until I'm supposed to meet Natalie for what will be the most boring movie. Grabbing two more beers, I hand them to Rob and Aaron and sit down to watch the Yankees game.

* * *

"THAT WAS THE LONGEST MOVIE OF MY LIFE." CROSSING MY
arms, I look over at Natalie. The lights have come on and I
can see her clearly for the first time in four hours. Reaching
over, I pick a kernel of popcorn from her red sweater and
throw it on the ground. "You did not tell me how long it was
going to be."

Natalie grins. "Now you're primed to watch the sequel.
It's six hours long." She points at the screen. "You can't tell
me you didn't like it."

"I did, actually. Now I understand why Rhett and Scar-
lett get mentioned in reference to epic romances—"

"Alongside your parents," Natalie looks at me pointedly
and stands. More popcorn tumbles to the floor. She brushes
the front of her jeans and looks at me expectantly.

Grumbling to myself, I stand and follow her out of the
theater. We both pause at the exit to pull on our jackets.

"Where to?" She looks at me expectantly.

I must be giving her a blank look, so she says, "You held
up your end of the bargain. Now it's my turn. But if you've
forgotten, we can just call it a night." She starts to turn away,
but I reach out and catch her.

"I haven't forgotten," I tell her, even though for a quick
moment I *did* forget what we're supposed to do after the
movie. "My place or yours?"

"Mine," she answers quickly. "Aaron can be so
annoying."

My mouth falls open, and she laughs. "Just kidding.
Aaron doesn't talk enough to be annoying." She purses her
lips and looks up. "Actually, that could become annoying
after a while. The never talking."

"It doesn't," I say, pushing open the door and holding it for her. She walks through, her hands immediately going to her pockets.

A stiff, cold wind blows down the block, whipping Natalie's long hair around her face. A section cuts across her face and catches on her lips. She tries spitting, but it's stuck in whatever makeup she's wearing on her lips. I reach out, removing the hair so she doesn't have to take her hands from her pockets.

"Thanks," she says, turning in the direction of her building.

I fall in step beside her, shoving my own hands into the front pockets of my jeans. It's really cold for November. As Rob would say, it's colder than a witch's tit. I keep that thought to myself. Considering the current political climate, it's not a good time to make comments like that. My mother would say it never was in the first place.

"How are your parents?" Natalie asks as we come to a stop at an intersection. We've just barely missed the walk sign. I would've pushed it, but Natalie stops when she knows it will soon switch to Don't Walk.

"You must be a mind reader. I was just thinking about my mom."

"I wish I were a mind reader. That would be cool." Natalie smiles. "So, how are they?"

"Good." I nod and shrug. "They're always good."

Natalie watches me, tipping her head to the side. I've always answered that question the exact same way, so she shouldn't be surprised to hear me say it again tonight. My parents have a perfect marriage, one that my mother made into a best-selling book nearly twenty years ago. That book was made into a movie, and the movie won an award. The entire world was in love with my parents' marriage. A popular book reviewer called it *Epic. Transcendent. The power of love at its finest.*

The progeny of such a union should be happily married by now, with a boy and a girl and a yellow Labrador Retriever. He shouldn't be on dating apps that are really just an excuse to have casual sex. Natalie attributes my proclivities to a cycle of extended adolescent rebellion that has now become a habit, and I let her. It's easier that way.

"No shock that your parents are perfect." Her voice is dreamy, and she doesn't notice me flinch at the word *perfect.* I hate that word. "Are you going there for Thanksgiving?"

"Yes. Are you doing the turkey day shuffle?" Poor Natalie. Her Thanksgiving is never about giving thanks. Mostly it's about Natalie splitting her time between two different houses and trying to have some semblance of a relaxing, enjoyable holiday. An enjoyable holiday can only be had if the company is enjoyable, and Natalie's parents are not. Her mom drinks too much wine and complains that her life hasn't turned out the way she envisioned. To be fair, it hasn't. The problem is that she places the blame for this on everybody else. Natalie's dad has a new wife and a five-year-old son. As hard as Natalie tries, she hasn't been able to feel comfortable in his new home.

Natalie groans, but the sound is mostly lost in the noise from the passing cars. "Yes, of course. Mom will attempt to stain the inside of her body with copious amounts of wine, and Dad will proudly present the Upgrades."

Even though it's fucking freezing outside, I remove my hand from my pocket and wrap it around Natalie's shoulders. She might say *Upgrade* like it doesn't bother her, but her dad's new family gutted her twice. Once when he remarried, and then again when his new wife announced her pregnancy. And they are definitely not upgrades. I can't speak for Natalie's mother, but Natalie is pinnacle. Paramount. Summit. Apex. Every synonym for highest point. The best friend in me rises to her defense, automatic and strong.

We maintain our pace down the street, but I lean in and tell her the words she so desperately needs to hear. "Your dad created a new family to fulfill something inside of him. He was not making up for a deficit with you."

She looks up at me, and in the lights from the oncoming cars I see the hint of moisture, the tears she refuses to shed. "Thank you," she whispers and leans her head on my shoulder. The embrace does not last longer than a few seconds. We are careful, so careful, not to touch for too long. Other than that stunt I pulled at brunch this morning, which probably only lasted about fifteen seconds, our touches do not linger. A thousand times we've heard the opinions of those who don't believe a guy and a girl can be best friends.

We have a thousand people to prove wrong.

7

NATALIE

The wine pools in my mouth, warm and spicy, and I let it stay there a moment longer before swallowing.

I hate talking about my dad. A divorce is one thing, but a whole new family? *Hey wound, it looks like you could use some salt.*

Aidan leans against my kitchen counter and reaches into his pockets, emptying them of his keys and wallet. The metal scrapes the counter as he pushes them away and hops up.

"You ready for that profile?" He sips his wine and raises one eyebrow.

I don't know how he makes that face. If I try to raise one eyebrow, I end up squinting one eye.

I make a sound, a cross between a grumble and a whine, and grab my laptop off the couch. Sitting down, I place my wine on the coffee table and open up the computer. Aidan settles next to me, sitting back against the couch and spreading his legs wide until his left knee bumps my right leg.

I offer him the laptop. I have no idea what website to type in. I know some are used for sex, but I think those might be apps. Feeling stupid, I grab my wine and feel the movement of my computer being taken from me.

Aidan types and a website pops up. He keys in a user-name and password and a new screen appears.

The screen has my name.

The screen has information about me.

The screen has my picture.

"Aidan, what the hell?" I look to Aidan, back to the computer, and back to Aidan again. He's watching me, waiting to see if he's in trouble. "You already created an account for me?"

"I had some free time today." His voice is even, but he's holding back a smile.

"Aidan…"

"What?"

A small sigh slips through my lips. "I don't know. It's not a big deal. I don't know why I'm making it one."

"Because you're uncomfortable and I've just taken you by surprise."

Settling back onto the couch, I prop my feet on the coffee table and lean over to get a closer look at my profile.

"Do you like it?" Aidan asks.

"Horseback riding?" I laugh as I say the words.

Aidan shrugs. "Good visual."

"Aidan!" My voice is part shock, part indignation.

"It's true, Nat."

"I'm not doing this to attract a guy who only wants to meet me because he likes the visual of me bouncing up and down on a horse." I almost cross my arms but catch myself. It's a habit leftover from my surly teenage years, and I don't care for it. Instead, I tuck one section of hair behind my ear and turn to face Aidan.

He looks at me, his expression challenging. "Don't give me the same look I'm giving you. If one of us doesn't cave, this becomes a stalemate. And that won't work, because I've already watched the worlds longest movie. Which means you" —he points at me with one finger— "have to cave."

My hair tickles my shoulders as my head shakes. "No to the horseback riding. It's ridiculous and not at all true."

"Fine. Perhaps you have a love of mechanical bull-riding."

"*No riding anything.*" Does this man need to see an ear doctor?

Aidan navigates to the edit box and deletes the words. "I only put that in there to push your buttons."

Reaching out, I grasp the skin beneath his upper arm in two fingers. He yelps and pushes my hand away.

"Do you want me to say that you're a romance author? Do you want a real profile?"

This isn't the way I pictured meeting someone, so I haven't put too much thought into the amount of honesty in my profile. Don't people usually lie on these things? Put your best foot forward and hide the baggage until you're actually dating, right? Get them hooked and then unpack the bags.

"What are you thinking about?" Aidan asks. His head is tipped to the side as he watches me.

"How honest I should be."

"Mostly honest, I think, if you're not only using this for hook-ups."

"I'm not."

Aidan starts typing. Leaning over, I read as he writes.

Author. Loves spicy Mexican food, beach vacations, and the Yankees.

"I don't watch basketball." I point needlessly at the word *Yankees.*

Aidan grimaces and opens his mouth, but I speak first. "I'm kidding. Of course I know the Yankees are a football team."

I smirk as he levels me with a dirty look and leans forward, setting the computer down on the table and picking up his glass of wine. "Your profile doesn't need to be completely true." He taps his glass against mine and sips from it. "What do you want to do now?"

I'm only half-listening. I've just realized I've never seen that picture of me.

"Where did you get that?" I nod my head at the open laptop.

"I took it last year in the park."

"I thought you were just pretending." My voice is a murmur.

"I was, mostly. And then you did that smirky thing you do, and I took a picture."

Looking back at the computer, I study my picture. Both corners of my mouth are turned up, but one much more so than the other. My eyes hold laughter, but not the loud kind.

I point at the computer. "Do I do that often?"

"Only to me."

Warmth spreads over my chest. I like that we have this. I like that he knows something like that about me, that he has noticed. It's nice to be seen.

Burrowing deeper into the couch cushions, I lean against him. The heat from his arm seeps into me. I've always loved how warm Aidan feels. His heat is comforting, like a sweater. It's a reminder of who I'm with, and that makes me happy.

"I'm going to use that in my next book." I tip my head, leaning it against his shoulder.

"Use what?" Aidan asks, his deep voice drifting down to me.

"The picture thing. It's sweet. Swoon-worthy, in fact."

"Don't thank me for that idea in your acknowledgments. It'll ruin my image." As he speaks, he makes his voice even deeper, a rich baritone.

"Surely you would drop dead if that happened."

"I might."

Aidan wiggles the arm I'm leaning on, so I sit up. Shifting, he wraps his arm around me and pulls me in close.

Not only is he warm like always, but he smells like he has since the day I met him. My college roommate said he smelled like sex, which was something I never understood. When I think of the scent of sex, I think of salty sweat and something that reminds me vaguely of bleach. Aidan smells like neither.

"What do you want to be when you're grown-up?" Aidan's question takes me off-guard.

"We're twenty-eight. Don't you think that qualifies as grown-up?"

"I live in a shoebox with two other guys. I think that excludes me from being an adult."

I sip my wine, then say "There's a difference between being an adult and being a grown-up. Turn eighteen, *bam,* adult. No questions asked. You can die for your country and be sent to prison. But grown-up... that's an obscure term."

"Does getting married make you an adult?"

I twist my lips as I think. "Maybe. Maybe not." I certainly

thought I was an adult when I accepted Henry's proposal. We were twenty-two and in love. At the time, love seemed like all we would need.

"You're an adult as defined by the constructs of the world." Aidan's voice trickles down around us. "You have a career, you've been divorced, you don't eat Cheetos for dinner." He taps my forearm with one finger. "Adult."

By that definition, I guess I am an adult. But I certainly don't feel like a grown-up. I feel like an unfinished thought, floating between good intentions and choices that were right at that moment. This isn't where I thought I would be by twenty-eight.

"Do you want another glass?" Aidan asks.

I nod and move so Aidan can get up. He comes back with the bottle and pours the remaining amount.

"You're going to have to change my profile again," I say, inclining my head toward his computer.

"Why?" he asks. My body shifts as he settles back down beside me.

"I'm a writer. Not an author."

He turns to face me. His eyes are dark, and his facial hair has grown in enough for two five o'clock shadows. "You've written a full manuscript. I've read it. I might be a math teacher, but I know good writing. Remember who my parents are?"

A blush sweeps my cheeks. Why is it so hard to hear this compliment?

He continues. "You're an author. Not a writer. And one day, you're going to be published. Your books are going to be everywhere, Natalie. Everywhere. I believe it with my whole fucking soul."

The first tear rolls down my cheek, and two more follow.

Aidan wipes them. "You're crying?"

I sniffle. "You're the one who said that nice stuff." A few more tears escape.

Aidan laughs. "Come here," he says, pulling me into his chest.

I snuggle in, the tears absorbed by his shirt.

"Best?"

"Hmm?" My voice is muffled.

"You're gonna make it."

Aidan might be talking about writing. He might be talking about life in general. Whichever one it is, it doesn't matter. His words are enough. Between his warm voice and sheer presence, Aidan has given me the same thing he has been giving me since that day in the recording studio: a safe place to be myself.

8

AIDAN

"Mom, hi." Cradling the phone between my shoulder and my ear, I dig my thermos of coffee from my bag. With a day full of teenagers ahead of me, I need to bathe in the liquid crack. At least it's Friday. Sweet Jesus, I'm ready for the weekend. And my date with Allison.

"Hello, darling." My mother's familiar voice fills my ear. She has always called me darling, but never *dah-ling*. Despite being richer than sin, she's not the *dah-ling* type.

"How's everything?" I ask, after taking a drink.

"Your father and I are good. How are you?"

"Status quo," I answer, fitting my thermos back into the little cupholder on the side of my bag. "Livin' the dream, yada yada."

The sound of my mother's clucking tongue fills my head with the image of her making the motion. It's what she does when she dislikes something I've said. "Life doesn't have to be status quo for you, Aidan."

Oh but it does, Mother.

"Uh huh," I say out loud. Agreeing with her is the easiest thing to do.

"You can find a nice girl any day now. You can..." She continues but I tune her out. I've heard this spiel a hundred times in the last few years. I think her grandma gene kicked in when she hit sixty. When she pauses to take a breath, I interject.

"Thanksgiving at four this year?" It's her favorite holiday, even more than Christmas. It's the best subject to use when I need to interrupt her.

"I can't believe it's only two weeks away." Excitement makes her voice tremble. "We're switching it up this year. Have to change things around to keep our lives fresh these days. Getting old sucks," she laughs. Automatically I begin to argue with her assessment of her age, but she continues right on as if I hadn't begun to speak. "We've decided to have Thanksgiving at the other house."

"Why aren't you having it at the apartment this year?" I ask, coming to a stop with a group of people on the corner as we wait for the light to turn. My parents' place on the Upper West Side is a little over the top, in my opinion, but they love it. The idea of staying at our place in Pound Ridge has me excited. I've always loved it there because it feels more like a home. When it was just the three of us there, I felt normal. My mom and dad cuddled in front of the fire and I'd pretend there were no secrets to keep.

"Your dad mentioned it might be nice to get out of the city for a few days, and I agreed. Oh, make sure you invite Natalie. Won't she be in the area at her mom or dad's place?

"I'll invite her."

"Good. How is she?"

"It's official," I tell her, my jaw tightening when I say it. I'd like to find Henry and punch him in the jaw.

"How is she handling it?"

The light turns green and I start walking. "As best as she can. She's more upset that her life isn't where she thought it would be."

"At least she didn't stay married to the wrong person."

"Yep," I say, my tone curt.

"Aidan—" my mom starts, but I cut her off.

"Not now, Mom."

"But Aidan," she tries again.

"I mean it, Mom. I don't want to start."

The line goes quiet. Glancing down at my phone, I see that she's still on the line. I feel guilty for talking to her like that. Sometimes it's hard to keep deep-seated irritation down in the depths.

"I'm almost to work. I'll ask Natalie if she can make it up for Thanksgiving."

"And the weekend," my mom adds. "You should both stay the weekend if you're going to come up."

"And the weekend," I echo.

"I love you, Aidan."

"I love you too," I say, hanging up.

A voice comes from behind. "Mr. Costa, was that your girlfriend?"

I start to turn, but Katy Simmons falls into step with me. If we weren't fifty feet from the entrance to the school, I'd make an excuse to hang back and let her walk in on her own. As a young, single male teacher, everything I do around the female students is under scrutiny. I get why, but it still sucks.

Looking down at Katy, I say, "Anyone ever told you it's rude to listen to other people's conversations?"

She rolls her eyes *and* her head, a feat only a teenager is capable of. "You're the one having a conversation with your girlfriend in public. It's not my fault I have working ears."

I nod and tuck my hands in my pockets. I've learned it's better not to answer my students' questions about my personal life. Keeps things cleaner that way. Katy spots a group of her friends and hurries after them. Briefly I consider reminding her that she better not be late to first period but decide against it. Natural consequences, and all that jazz. I make my way to the teacher's lounge to refill my thermos, then on to my classroom. Natalie's text comes through just as the first bell rings.

Someone sent me a message.

I type out a quick response. **Text? Email? Hedwig?**

Natalie: From the dating app. Where's the annoyed best friend emoji? Love the Harry Potter reference.

My classroom door opens and three boys walk in as I finish typing out my text. **The annoyed best friend emoji can be found to the left of the whale and above the cactus.**

Looking up, I say, "Hey guys, good morning." My greeting is met with grumbles and bleary eyes.

Natalie: Very funny. I'm freaking out. What do I say?

I have about ten more seconds to devote to Natalie's non-crisis, and then I need to put my phone in my desk. Quickly, I tell her to act normal and do not mention her recent divorce.

Katy scoots in just as the last bell rings. She smirks and says, "Bet you thought I was going to be late." Shaking my head, I set my phone in my desk and tell my students to get out their textbooks. They groan, like always, and like always, this baffles me. They know what's coming. Every day we go through the lesson, they come to the board, and I assign homework. Why bother complaining when they know exactly what's going to happen?

* * *

"WHAT DO YOU DO FOR EXERCISE? YOU SEEM SO FIT." HER voice travels across the table at the same time as her hand. Her fingers graze the top of my hand and linger, curling over my skin with a feather-light touch.

"I run, mostly, and use an app." I know Allison doesn't really care about my response.

Leaning forward across the small table, I ask, "What do you do for exercise?"

Allison smiles, sex dripping from the slightly upturned corners of her mouth. "Oh, this and that," she says, in a voice meant to take me to wherever it is she does *this and that*.

"Interesting," I say, finishing my scotch. "I've never heard of that type of exercise.

Allison's fingers slip from my hand and up my forearm. Licking her lips, she says, "I could show you."

I open my mouth at the same time my pocket vibrates. Reaching down, I pull out the phone partway and see a number I don't know. "Sorry," I mutter, smiling apologetically at Allison and tapping the button to answer.

"Hello?"

"Is this Aidan?" a man's gruff voice asks.

"Yeah. Who's this?" I sit back in my seat and look around the small bar, as though the caller is nearby.

"I own a bar on 73rd. There's a girl here who's shit-faced.

She dropped her phone on the way back to the bathroom and you're listed as her emergency contact."

I shake my head and palm the stubble on my jaw.

"I can call someone else," he says.

"No," I bark, then in a normal voice, I say, "I'm coming. What's the name of the place?"

"Sassy Maiden. There's a mermaid on the sign out front."

The line goes dead. I sigh, looking across at Allison as I slip the phone back into my pocket.

"You have to go," she says, her sexy voice gone.

I nod.

She looks away, and after a moment looks back at me. "That was a pretty obvious bail call."

I shake my head. "That was not a bail call."

"Yeah, right." She stands. It's a good thing her white wine is gone because I have the feeling I'd be wearing it if there were any left. "Next time you send an SOS, tell your friend to call with a more elaborate story." She yanks her purse off the corner of her chair with such force that the chair teeters for a moment before crashing into the ground. People turn to look and are met with my sheepish face. Standing, I throw a couple twenties down, stop to right the fallen chair, and stride out of one bar in search of another bar with a mermaid sign.

"Where is she?" I ask the first bartender who looks my way. There are three behind the bar, two of whom are women wearing white mesh long sleeve T-shirts and hot pink bras underneath.

"The drunk girl?" the blonde asks as the brunette reaches around her for a glass.

"Yes," I say, thinking of how much fun it will be to tease Natalie about this later.

"I checked on her a few minutes ago," the brunette says, pouring vodka into a shaker. "She's sitting on the floor in the bathroom." She walks off to the other end of the bar and grabs something else to pour into her shaker.

"Great," I mutter. This is not how my night was supposed to go.

The blonde watches me, her face uncertain. Whatever she's thinking about, she seems to make up her mind because she inclines her head toward the back of the place. "Bathrooms are that way. I don't know what happened to the guy she was here with."

My eyebrows draw together at the mention of a guy. What guy? Natalie just got her first message from the app this morning. She wouldn't already be meeting him, would she? Rookie mistake.

"Your girlfriend didn't look happy. With that guy, I mean. Maybe it wasn't a date." The blonde bartender is speaking again, and she obviously feels bad for telling on Natalie. Normally I would correct her mistake about Natalie being my girlfriend, but right now I need to step foot into a place I have no desire entering.

"Thanks," I tell her, and move away, weaving through the crammed tables until I get to the women's restroom. Three girls stand in line and one of them yells "Hey!" after I push open the door and slip inside. A girl stands at the mirror, leaning over and applying something to her lips, and in the mirror's reflection I see a mass of dark hair spilling over onto the tile.

Striding over to the crouched figure on the floor, I bend down and say softly, "Best?"

"Go away," comes the muffled response.

"Okay," I say, moving to stand.

"Don't go," Natalie yells, her arm shooting out to stop me. She lifts her head from her knees and looks at me. Her eye makeup has run all over and her nose is red. If she were in a laughing mood, I'd tell her Halloween was a couple weeks ago.

"I'm here," I say, crouching down again. She leans her head on my arm.

"It didn't go well," she says, sniffling.

"I gathered that," I respond, meeting eyes with two of the girls who'd been in line. One gives me a dirty look, the other makes a sympathetic face. "Let's get out of here." Wrapping an arm around Natalie's shoulders, I haul her to her feet. Her first step is wobbly, so I keep my arm firmly around her. It's no easy task getting Natalie around the tables and to the front door.

"Hey," a voice shouts out above the noise. It's the blonde bartender, and she's waving Natalie's phone in her hand. Changing directions, I haul Natalie over to the bar.

"No more booze," Natalie complains weakly.

The bartender laughs and hands me the phone. I thank her and she glances at Natalie, who's doing a terrible job shifting from one foot to the other. "Good luck," she says and turns to pour a beer.

With Natalie's phone safely stored in my pocket, I steer her out of the place. We're four steps out of the bar when Natalie begins to shiver violently.

"Shit," I mutter, realizing she doesn't have a coat. Her dress is something better suited for the summer, with a bunch of complicated straps, and a healthy amount of cleavage.

Slipping off my coat, I drape it over her shoulders. She looks at me gratefully, but her teeth are still chattering. I nod and try not to acknowledge that I'm the one freezing my ass off now. Pulling Natalie to the edge of the sidewalk, I raise a hand into the oncoming lights. After a moment a cab pulls over and I open the door, practically shoving Nat inside. I slide in beside her and give her address to the guy. He nods, but otherwise, he's silent the entire drive, and so is Natalie. Her head is tipped back against the seat, and I peer over, closing most of the darkened space to try and see if she's sleeping.

"Don't even think about putting the moves on me, Mr. Teacher." Natalie's voice is surprisingly clear for her level of intoxication. She continues, "I'm not one of your app girls."

I snort. "Weren't you an app girl tonight?"

She flashes me a dirty look and looks pointedly out her window. The car pulls to the curb in front of Natalie's building and I hop out, hurry around the back of the cab, and open her door. I offer my hand, but she ignores it and ends up bumping her head on the top of the doorframe.

"Ouch," she half yells, half wails.

"Come on." Pulling her into my side, I help her all the way to the door and to the elevator. She slouches against the wall while I punch in her floor number.

When the elevator door opens, Natalie stumbles past me, tapping the tip of my nose on her way. "You're a gem, Aidan, you know that?"

I follow her to number 708, then redirect her to where she lives at 716, and take the keys from her. As soon as the door is open Natalie makes a beeline for the bathroom. In seconds I hear the unmistakable heaves and moans of a person retching.

Fuck my life. I'm supposed to be with Allison right now. Hopefully she'll believe me when I tell her why our date was cut short. I know I could just find another person to spend my free time with, but I actually like Allison. Not *like* like, but her personality is tolerable both in and out of the bedroom.

Lifting my hand, I knock on the bathroom door. It swings open, and Natalie crawls back over to the toilet. She throws up once more and sits against the wall, wiping the back of one hand across her mouth.

Her eyes are wide and round, glassy, but she's regarding me with such curiosity. A strap from her dress hangs off one shoulder, laying haplessly against her upper arm. Her beauty is unmarred by the mascara smeared below her eyes. Natalie has always been achingly beautiful.

"What?" I ask her, leaning into the room but staying at the threshold. One hand grips the round door handle, the other is on the top of the door jamb.

"Nothing," she murmurs, but her eyes don't leave me.

"Say it," I tell her. I know she won't say anything, because she's terrible at following directions, especially when they come from me. But tonight, perhaps because she's shit faced, she speaks.

"I'm not like your app girls, am I?"

I don't understand her question, but I hear Natalie's tone. What I can't comprehend is *why* Natalie sounds sad. Right now probably isn't the best time to ask.

Pointing at the multi-colored new addition on the front of her dress, I say "Some of it missed the toilet." The longer I look, the more I see just how much of it missed the toilet. It's on her right forearm and her left leg.

Natalie glances down and scrunches her nose. "Gross," she mutters and grabs for a handful of toilet paper. She mops up her skin as the sound of the spinning roll of toilet paper slows. When she's finished, she tosses the toilet paper in the toilet and uses her foot to flush, then scoots back and puts her forehead on her knees in the same way I first found her in the bar.

Leaving my post at the door, I walk past Natalie and sit on the edge of the tub. I reach over and turn the nozzle, then slide the plug into the drain. In my shower, there is only one bottle and it washes me from head to toe. Natalie's shower is a different story. I pick through bottles of shampoo and conditioner, deep conditioner and body wash, and other things that don't make sense to me (what the hell is a body bar?) until I find bubble bath.

Natalie doesn't look up until the bath is half full and the suds are mountainous.

"You used too much soap," she says, standing. "But it looks amazing."

If her eye makeup was messed up before, it looks even worse now. Black mascara streaks down her cheeks like some kind of Native American warrior. Has she been crying? I was sitting right there, but the sounds of the running water must've covered it.

She must know what she looks like, because without looking in the mirror above the sink Natalie turns on the faucet and begins washing her face. I focus on not over-flowing the world's sudsiest bath, and when I look at her again, she looks more like the Natalie I know.

"I promise I looked pretty earlier before I had too much to drink."

Staring up at her from the edge of the tub, I tell her the truth without a second thought. "You look beautiful right now, too."

She ducks her chin, but I see the little smile playing at the edge of her lips. She turns away from the sink and teeters. I'm up instantly, crossing the small space and steadying her with my hands on her arms.

"I didn't think you had any alcohol left in you," I joke.

"A little light-headed, that's all. It always happens after I throw up."

"Right." I nod. I was going to leave and let her bathe, but that's not a good idea if she's light-headed.

Natalie's mind must be where mine is because she looks at me sheepishly and says, "Would you stay with me while I'm in the bath?"

I nod again because I don't know what to say. Sitting with her while she's in the bath is definitely crossing one of our invisible lines. I glance at the bath. There are so many bubbles, she'll be completely covered.

She turns slowly, my hands dropping from her arms as she rotates. Moving her hair aside with one hand, she asks, "Can you please unzip me? I can't reach. I twisted myself into a pretzel trying to get it on."

I stare at the top of the shiny black zipper, confused. "Savannah isn't back until tomorrow and you wore a dress you can't unzip yourself?"

Natalie stays quiet, and then it dawns on me. "Nat, were you planning on, uh," I pause and cough on the words. Quickly my brain comes up with a sentence that doesn't include the word *fuck*. "Were you planning on not being the one to unzip this dress?"

"Please don't say anything," Natalie whispers. Her voice is filled with mortification.

So I don't. Wordlessly, I reach for the black zipper and pull it down. Down past her upper back, beyond the line where a bra should be but isn't, and all the way to the very bottom of her lower back.

Natalie steps around me and to the edge of the tub. I turn around, and the sound of fabric falling down reaches me. I tip my chin up to the ceiling, but in the process of doing so, I've forgotten about the mirror above the sink.

I should look away. I know I should. But I can't. Frozen, I watch as Natalie steps from the pile of clothes at her feet and places one foot in the tub. Her second foot follows, and she sinks down below the bubbles.

A quiet, appreciative moan slips from her. "Thank you, Aidan."

"No problem," I cough out the second word and turn around. Where are my insides right now? Where is my brain? What has happened to my body? I feel like a violently shaken snow globe.

Natalie makes a splashing sound and it jolts me from trying desperately to recognize even an inch of myself. Lowering the lid of the toilet, I sink down onto it and *finally* drag my eyes to hers.

She's watching me with that same look from earlier, only this time the curiosity is mixed with something brought to her by the ebbing of alcohol. I can practically see the words dancing on the tip of her tongue.

I want to look away from her, look anywhere but at the familiar face of my best friend that now has the image of her naked body to go with it. "Are you going to say it?" I ask, gruffer than I intended.

"Sometimes I wonder... why not us, Aidan?" Fear takes over her face and her lower lip trembles. I know how hard it is for her to say these words because it's almost as difficult for me to hear them. Anger fills my chest. I despise this secret I keep. Despise how it has taken from me the chance to be normal like Natalie, robbed me of the opportunity to make mistakes and fall in love.

"You know me, Nat. I'm not a commitment guy." I hate these words. I hate them even more because right now, they feel like an even bigger lie than the one I've been covering up all these years.

"And I'm a commitment girl," she echoes, swiping at some bubbles and flicking them off her hand. She bites her lower lip and sinks down below the bubbles until her whole head disappears. After a few seconds, she pops back up, her hair slicked down her head.

"I'm done," she says, sticking out one arm.

I'm certain that's the shortest bath in the history of baths, but I don't say that. I grab a towel from the rack and hand it to her. She starts to stand, but I stop her. "Hang on, let me leave the room."

She says something, but I'm hustling from the room and the sounds of the sloshing water make it hard to hear. Settling on the gray sofa, I look out the window and try to tune out the sounds coming from beyond the open bathroom door. I know when she has stepped from the tub, I know when she has dried off, but it's quiet and I don't know what she has been doing for the last minute, and it has the contents of my stomach on a teeter-totter. Will she be dressed when she comes out here? What if she's dabbing perfume in all the right places? Is she planning to take us to a place we've never dared to go? Natalie's mirrored image slams back into my thoughts, how soft her skin looked as she gingerly climbed into the tub. *Why not us, Aidan?*

A moment later she emerges from the bathroom, her hair wrapped in a towel and a second towel covering her body. Two different and distinct emotions flood my body. My brain doesn't understand the disappointment I feel, but my heart does. My heart doesn't understand the relief I feel, but my brain does.

"Thanks for coming to save me," she says, gliding past me and to the front door. In all our years of friendship, this might be the first time she has made it clear I need to leave.

"Thanksgiving," I blurt out as I stand up from the couch, and her hand pauses on the lock. "Pound Ridge house. My mom's having it there this year. She wants you to come and stay the weekend, if you can."

Natalie turns to face me. "We're both supposed to be at a wedding up there on the Saturday after Thanksgiving, remember? Malachi and Karis?"

It sounds familiar, but right now I don't have the patience to search my memory. I threw out the invitation when Natalie said she would respond for us.

She takes in my blank face and keeps going. "Tell your mom I said yes. Saves me from having to get a hotel." Natalie is back to being Natalie, like her question in the tub never happened.

She opens the front door and gazes at me. "I'm sorry I kept you out so late. Good thing it wasn't on a school night."

"You get a detention," I say, trying for a joke, but it's forced and not at all funny. Still, Natalie laughs because she knows she is supposed to.

I cross the apartment and pass her, praying I don't succumb to the amazing scent coming off her skin.

"See you soon," I say once I'm safely in the hall and no longer trapped by whatever that amazing bubble bath was. Now it smells like stale air and all the different dinners people cooked tonight. I drag in a deep breath of it in an attempt to clear my senses.

"Lunch?" she offers. She knows this is weird.

"Lunch," I echo, then turn and leave. She closes the door before I get to the elevator.

While the elevator takes its sweet time, I look up at the ceiling and take a deep breath.

What the hell happened in there?

9

NATALIE

My hands shake as I type. Maybe I should quit chugging caffeine.

Or maybe they're only performing a perfectly synchronized dance with what's going on inside my body.

Why not us, Aidan?

What possessed me to say that? Not drunkenness, because I was mostly sober by then.

I haven't heard from Aidan in three days. For us, that's a lot of time. Too much. I've spooked him. We had an unspoken but mutually understood deal, and I broke it. I brought up *us*, as though the possibility of such even existed, and I don't even know why.

My bad date sounds like a good place to lay the blame. Matthew Robertson was not six foot two, like his profile said. He stood two inches taller than my five foot five height. I didn't like his hands. Sausage-like fingers and hairy knuckles flew through the air as he described his job and why he believed he was too good for it.

My first gin and tonic was meant to loosen my screwed-up shoulders.

My second was to quell my growing irritation with my date.

My third was because *why the hell not?* I was on a bad date. My very first bad date, in fact. A third drink seemed like a good way to celebrate. I sipped from my glass, the ice fell against my upper lip, and I silently toasted two men: my date, for giving me the experience, and Henry, for making it possible in the first place.

There were no good reasons for drinks four and five. I was drunk, and that's that. Matthew left during drink four, immediately after I told him I'm recently divorced. Apparently ape hands are acceptable to him, but a divorce is a non-starter. It was probably the tears that spooked him, but how was I supposed to not get a little misty-eyed? I'm not a robot.

Drink five hardly graces my memory. One second I was getting up to go to the bathroom, the next I was walking into the chilly night with Aidan by my side.

He'd cared for me, the same way he always does. My rock, my steady, my best friend. Heaven help me if he ever gets a girlfriend. Not being number one in his life just might kill me. I know how unfair that is. He watched me get married. He stood on the other side of Henry, a groomsman only because that was back when Henry still cared about making me happy.

Why not us, Aidan?

Regret fills me. I want to lay my head on my keyboard and let the side of my face fill in this spreadsheet.

Years of knowing Aidan has taught me that he really, truly doesn't want anything to do with relationships. We work because I'm safe, and three nights ago, just by saying those four words, I turned myself into a risk. I want to apologize, but I don't know how. A small part of me feels indignant and wants the question answered. *Why? Why not us?*

Aidan has never tried. Not once, not even that first day when I foolishly brought him home and he discovered the ugly secret lying beneath the shiny, virtuous veneer of my life.

Savannah's voice is suddenly near my ear, her accent thick from her visit home. She arrived back in NYC three days ago, saying *y'all* and *darlin'* in a voice thicker than molasses. As time passes, she will slowly lose the twang, like water dripping from a slow leak. I'd hugged her tightly when she walked in the door. Her appearance made me realize I'd been lonely.

"Spin tonight?" Her whispered question tickles my ear. We work in a quiet office, and all conversation takes place in hushed tones. Savannah smacks her backside and immediately we're the recipients of two interested gazes. "My mama is an angel, but I swear she has a little bit of devil hidden down deep. The woman fries everything and force feeds me."

"The nerve," I say, feigning shock. "Force fed by your own mother."

"It's a travesty. To my thighs, anyway." Savannah does a weird chicken dance without flapping her arms, trying to make her thighs move. "See? She put jiggle in my wiggle."

I snort, trying like hell to keep my laughter contained. "Spin tonight," I nod, attempting to be serious. Lord knows I could use the distraction.

"I'm inviting Charity and Mari, too." Savannah backs

away from my desk as she talks, and as I watch she walks first to Charity's desk, then a few minutes later to Mari's.

Dipping my head, I bury myself in my work, where I stay for the remainder of the afternoon.

* * *

"THAT WAS GOOD, WASN'T IT?" CHARITY WIPES AT HER SWEATY forehead with a pink towel.

"So good," Savannah agrees, red-faced and breathless. She had a much harder time with the climbs than the rest of us. She offers me an arm. "Smell that? It's the scent of fried chicken seeping from my pores."

I make a face and push her arm away. I can handle almost anything, but not sweat. Savannah knows this, and so she loves to torture me.

"Who wants a burrito?" Mari asks as we head out of the studio. When three sets of shocked expressions meet hers, she adds, "What? Don't tell me you all don't want a burrito right now."

"Kind of, yeah," I admit.

Charity raises a hand. "Me too."

Savannah sighs. "Assholes." Her arms slowly slides into the air above her head. "Me three."

Mari leads the way to a food truck and orders four Gringas, two spicy and two mild. When they're ready, she hands a spicy to me, keeps one for herself, and we cheers the foil-wrapped goodness. The other two grab theirs and we stand there, eating like we haven't had a decent meal in a week.

"Is your divorce final?" Charity asks, keeping her gaze on me while she takes a bite.

"Um hmm," I manage to say around a mouthful. Even though I wanted the divorce, even though my lungs longed to take a full breath the entire time last year we were married, the question slices through me.

"Am I allowed to ask that question?" Charity looks concerned.

"Too late," I reply, taking another bite. The warmth in my hand decreases as the burrito dwindles.

Mari laughs. "What's next for you? You're single now. Any man catching your eye?"

Instead of answering, I take another huge bite. My mouth is so full they will grow bored waiting for me to chew and hopefully move on to another topic. One that doesn't include whatever is next for me. Why are all milestones quickly followed by a *next*? You got engaged? *When is the wedding?* You got married? *When are you having a baby?* You had a baby? *When are you giving the baby a sibling?* And on and on and on.

It worked. They've moved on to discussing relationship fails. Everyone but Savannah, anyway. Drew has been her boyfriend for six years and they appear to be nothing but solid, despite the fact they choose not to live together or get married. They are happy to just be where they are.

"Look at that couple." Charity looks at something beyond me.

"Aw. Look at the way she's gazing up at him."

Reluctantly I turn around, my eyes searching through the moving people until they land on two stationary figures. They face each other, and the girl tips her head back slightly, exposing her neck, sending a coquettish smile up at... Aidan. *Oh my god*. My bottom lip peels away from my upper, and I taste the cold air. My stomach feels the opposite. It's more like a fire was lit within me. Seeing Aidan in an awkward morning-after scenario is one thing, but I've never seen him out with a woman. I've never seen the before, only the after. The before Aidan is charming. He's smiling down at her, but only one side of his mouth is turned up. It's... well, I don't like it. Nor do I like these feelings. *Territorial. Jealous. Comparing.* She's blonde. Of course she is. He prefers them. I think this is the same woman from the day I picked him up for brunch. She's tiny and looks delicate, like she should be ice skating or pirouetting on the inside of a little girl's jewelry box.

I wish I wasn't seeing this. I wish the whole world would disappear and I was on my couch, watching TV. I wish I never would've asked that pointless question.

"Natalie?"

Fuck.

"Aidan, hi." I say his name like I'm surprised to see him. The pulling together of his eyebrows tells me he knows I'm faking.

People walk between us and I'm hoping when they pass Aidan will be gone, swept away by the sea of coats.

No such luck. He's still there, and his eyes are bright, panic dancing inside them as he contemplates his next move. Squaring his shoulders, he winds a hand around his date and leads her to us.

"Natalie, this is Allison." Aidan gestures from me to her then turns to her. "Natalie is my best friend." The tension in her facial muscles relaxes.

No, Allison, I'm not a threat to you and whatever it is you two are going to do tonight.

Aidan says hello to Savannah and jokes that her hair is bigger since she came back. Mari and Charity haven't met

Aidan, so I introduce them, and then... well, there's not much else to say. The awkward silence stretches on and I have the insane desire to scream and stomp, shout and dance, because suddenly I'm filled with this bizarre energy and it's pulsing through my drained, exhausted limbs. Aidan's gaze is on me, and he's doing that thing where he tries to read me. He looks confused as if maybe I'm a book and my sentences are jumbled, and I feel a childish sense of pleasure at not being so easily read.

"So," I start.

"Well," Aidan says at the same time.

But I'm not waiting for whatever he's going to say. "Enjoy your night." I fake smile at Aidan, and then tell Allison it was nice to meet her.

Aidan smiles tightly, nods at my friends, and turns around, his arm still around Allison. They walk away, and Allison resumes the game they are playing, the one where she gazes up at him like he's a god. *He picks his nose at stoplights. He says he's not doing it, but he totally is. When he was little, he thought he was Aquaman and jumped into a pool without knowing how to swim. His mom jumped in after him and he was pissed because she'd ruined his fun.*

Mari's voice jumps into my head. "Girl." She lays a hand on my shoulder. "What the hell was that?"

I eye her. "What?"

"That man is your best friend?"

I nod.

"Since when is a man and woman best friends?"

"We've been friends since high school."

"That's when you were a girl and he was a boy."

I laugh, but the sound is empty. "And what? Now he's a man?"

She lifts her head and brings it back down slowly. "Precisely."

"He's not my type, Mari. That's why we work. That girl you just met?" With my thumb, I gesture behind me in the direction they went. "He met her on an app. They are going to have sex. He won't see her for longer than a month, two at the most. That's what he does." I shrug. "That's what he has *always* done."

Mari makes no attempt to hide the skepticism in her eyes. "For someone who only fucks for fun, he seemed very interested in how you were *feeling*."

With a wave of my hand, I dismiss her words. "He's not an unfeeling asshole. He's actually very kind. He doesn't" — holding up my fingers I air quote— "*fuck for fun* because he's a jerk."

"Then why does he?" Savannah asks.

My mouth opens as if I have an answer, but really I have nothing to say. My head shakes. "I don't know."

"Childhood trauma," Charity says, smacking her lips and chewing her last bite. She rolls the foil from her burrito into a ball and tosses it into a nearby garbage can.

"No." I shake my head. "No childhood trauma. His parents are the personification of perfect. Remember the book *For You I Will*?"

Mari and Savannah nod. Charity says, "I only saw the movie. But" —she pretends to drive a knife into her chest— "oh my god, I cried like a baby. Best romance I've ever seen."

"I think it's universally agreed upon that was the best love story of our generation. And Aidan's mother wrote it." Three shocked expressions look back at me. "It's based upon her relationship with his dad."

"No," Mari gasps, grabbing ahold of my forearm. "The

marriage of convenience when she was actually in love with him, but he was in love with the other girl?"

"He wasn't in love with the other girl," Savannah breaks in. "He was in lust. And the other girl didn't truly love him back. That's why Grace married Alejandro. So he could stay in the country and pursue his feelings for the other girl. She loved him enough to sacrifice for his happiness." A gargled sound comes from the back of her throat. "We have to stop talking about it. I'm going to cry."

"You know how it ends," I remind her. "They fell in love, made a baby, and lived happily ever after."

Mari looks over my shoulder as if Aidan is still visible. "And that was the baby they made? Dammmn they did a good job. He's dark, like his father. Wait." She holds out a hand, her face serious. "Is Alejandro really Venezuelan?"

I can't help but laugh. "Yes, he is. A lot of the story is accurate."

Charity stomps her feet on the ground and crosses her arms in front of herself. "Can we go somewhere warm and dissect how gorgeous Aidan is?"

"Nope," I say quickly. "It's time for this girl to go home. Savannah?" I turn to her. She nods and gives both Charity and Mari quick goodbye hugs.

We make it three blocks when Savannah starts talking. "Don't take this the wrong way, but the way Aidan looked at you tonight... well, Henry never did that."

"I'm not sure what look you're talking about, but you only knew me when Henry and I were failing." I feel the need to point this out, to defend Henry in some weird sort of way. Maybe I'm not defending him, but our marriage. I don't fucking know.

Savannah doesn't respond, so I look at her. She's staring at me pointedly.

I sigh. I know what she wants me to ask. "How did Aidan look at me?"

"Like your breath was more important than his own."

I roll my eyes and shake my head. "Oh please. Have you been reading my romance novels?"

"No. I mean, yeah, a little. But only the sexy parts."

My hands fly into the air. "Only the sex? Seriously?" There's no way I'm telling her about my most recent declination.

"That's not the point. We were talking about Aidan."

"What about him?"

"I've seen you guys together, what, twenty times? And you've always acted like permanent fixtures in one another's friend zones. Like little statues. But tonight—" Savannah lifts her hands the same time as her shoulders, then she drops them. "Tonight it looked like maybe your stone is crumbling and you were actually being human. *Both* of you."

"I didn't do anything."

Savannah lets out a short burst of a laugh. "Yeah. Sure. You didn't look like someone popped out from behind a tree and yelled boo."

"I was surprised, that's all." My voice is a murmur. "I've never seen him on an actual date. I was caught off-guard."

"If you say so." Savannah steps into our building and I follow. We make it all the way up to our apartment without another word and I'm grateful. Talking about Aidan is low on the list of things I want to do right now.

After an hour of sitting on the sofa watching HGTV, I say goodnight and go to my room. I'm physically exhausted from the spin class and emotionally exhausted from feeling awkward around my best friend. The second my head hits the pillow, my mind begins to wander. I can't stop seeing the way Allison looked up at Aidan. So flirtatious. So bold. So ready for whatever was next for them.

Did they take it slow? Or was it fast and hot? Did they make it all the way back to his place or did he pull her into a dark alley and start there?

How long has it been since I've had sex? *A long freaking time.*

Henry was the second person I had sex with, and there was a time when I thought he would be my last. Unlike his sometimes harsh personality, in bed, he was gentle and kind. Unless he'd had too much to drink. Then he was rougher, whispering things into my ear he'd never say otherwise.

Maybe it's because I miss Henry, or what he represented.

Maybe it's because I know Aidan is getting some tonight and I'm alone *again.*

Or maybe my hand slips over my abdomen and into the waistband of my pajama pants because it's been *so long.*

A young Henry floats through my head. He's high from a win on the football field, drunk at an after-party with his arm around my shoulders. I'm half-drunk too and high on knowing I'm his girl. The football god and the dancer. Picture perfect. The scene floats around me, and my present self knows what my past self doesn't. That night, Henry and I will fall asleep together, and in the morning we'll have sex for the first time, and he'll take me to a high I'd never experienced before.

My body welcomes the memory, and my shoulders relax as my thigh muscles tighten.

Putting the scene on replay in my head, I let go completely and hope to reach the same high I experienced that morning. My brain, however, remembers what happened after, and it won't let me press the replay button one more time. As hard as I fight it, the scene keeps going and now I'm in the kitchen of Henry's apartment. I've just come from his room and I'm wearing his T-shirt only. I wouldn't have walked out, but I was parched. Aidan is in the kitchen, shirtless, standing in front of the open fridge and drinking milk from the container. He takes in my appearance, says nothing, but offers me the milk. I walk closer, accept the milk, drink, and wipe the back of my hand across my lips. Aidan takes it from me and puts it back in the fridge. Drawing me in with one arm, he tucks me into his side and lays a cheek on top of my head.

"You okay?" His voice floats down around me, and I know that he knows what Henry and I did.

"Yes." My voice is small.

"That's all that matters."

Henry appears a moment later and frowns at us. I jump away, but Aidan doesn't move. We hadn't been doing anything, but our close proximity feels wrong. Maybe it was the fact Aidan and I only made one whole outfit combined. It could have been Aidan's ridiculous body, with abs that rippled like water rescinding over sand. That morning, I took Henry's outstretched hand and let him lead me to his bedroom. I didn't look back, but I've always wondered what the look on Aidan's face was.

Henry is gone from my head. Aidan takes his place, and my hand stills. This is wrong, but it's bad in a delicious way. My hand moves, and in my head, it's Aidan's hand moving over me. Aidan, with his lopsided smile, lies beside me in my bed and reaches down.

My phone pings and a light glows from my nightstand. With my free hand, I reach over and peer at the screen, shock rolling through me for a second time tonight.

Aidan: Hi.

Panicked, I look around my room as if somehow I've been caught. There is nothing there but darkness and the glow of the moon peeking around the drawn curtains. Slowly sliding my hand from my pants, I wipe it across my comforter and start typing.

Hey. Date over already?

Aidan: The date ended shortly after I saw you.

The alley. I knew it.

Never took you for a minute man.

Aidan responds with the middle-finger emoji, then the three dots appear, so I wait for more.

Aidan: You looked disappointed when I saw you tonight.

Disappointed in what?

Aidan: Me.

Hardly.

Aidan: In what, then?

I wasn't disappointed. Just surprised.

Aidan: Gotcha.

He doesn't say anything else. Three dots don't appear. I wait five minutes, then turn off my phone.

In the darkness of my room, I reach back down and bring myself to the high I was seeking. I christened my new bed all by my damn self.

10

AIDAN

THIS IS EXACTLY WHAT I NEEDED. COLD BEER, GREASY BAR food, and the Yankees on every TV in my vicinity.

"We'll have another round," Rob tells the girl who dropped off our baskets of burgers. With a full mouth, I stare at the screen closest to me. It's the bottom of the ninth and we're tied four-four with the Dodgers. I want this win more than I've wanted anything in my life. In this moment, anyway.

Finishing my bite, I wash it down with the dregs of my beer and grab a handful of fries. Just as I toss them in my mouth, Rob utters one of those information seeking sentences I would rather ignore.

"Best hasn't been around much lately."

A caveman-like grunt winds its way around my mouthful of fries, but it doesn't deter Rob.

"Thought with her divorce she'd be around a lot more."

"Why do you care so much? Do you want to date her? Break the rule?" My voice is sullen. I wipe my mouth with a paper napkin and ball it up, then toss it on the table.

Rob glances at me, then back to the screen. "Maybe. She's cute. She has that smart-girl vibe. The older I get, the more I appreciate smart girls."

"I was kidding," I mutter, beyond grateful for the fresh round of beers the server is dropping off. Grabbing mine, I drink until it's half gone.

"So was I," Rob says, loudly clapping my back three times. My shoulders curl in each time his hand comes down. "I mean, yeah, Best is a catch, but I know better. So do you, obviously, because you won't move beyond the friend-zone."

Rob is right that I know better and wrong that Natalie is cute. She's not *cute.* She's beautiful. Her lower lip is bigger than her top, and in the center of her upper lip is a 'V' shape so pronounced it looks like the top of a heart. Her nose is slightly upturned, and her eyes are wide and round so that she always looks like she's interested in what's happening. Her eyes are the opposite of mine. According to Natalie, my squinty eyes make me appear to be perpetually brooding. I certainly am right now. Listening to Rob talk about Natalie, serious or not, doesn't help my mood.

"I told you what the deal was the first day you met Natalie. We're best friends, and that's it." I stare at the screen as I talk, and watch the Dodgers hit the ball deep into the outfield. My breath sticks in my throat until the ball lands safely in the glove of the outfielder.

"She's divorced now. I think the rules you've always abided by have changed."

"I'm her best friend, not some asshole who wants to jump her bones because she no longer wears a ring on her finger."

"Who said anything about jumping her bones? I was talking about you getting yourself a real girlfriend."

"You know I don't date."

Rob gulps his beer and sets it back down. "I guess I was holding out hope that you were waiting for Natalie to be free from that dickhead."

Despite my irritation at Rob, I laugh. Rob never liked Henry. It didn't help that the first time they met, Henry took one sip of his beer and sent it back, complaining it was too 'hoppy.' Henry was at a disadvantage after that, and every time he talked over Natalie or interrupted her, his stock fell lower and lower.

Rob wanted me to talk to Natalie about Henry, but I refused. The fastest way to hurt our friendship would've been to tell Natalie her husband was an ass. I learned my lesson the hard way almost a year after she began dating Henry when I told her she needed to look past the good boy side-parted hair, perfect teeth, and hero-like, big man on campus status. She'd stalked away from me, refused to answer my call for three weeks, and that was when I learned that Natalie wanted to recreate what her parents should've had. *The perfect marriage.* When all you can see are external characteristics, you can begin to match them up like puzzle pieces.

You're single. Me too. We fit.

You want kids? Me too. We fit.

One day you want to leave the city and settle down in a nice suburb? Me too. We fit.

On and on and on it goes, until soon you're thinking the words *match made in heaven.*

But what happens when the external dries out, then

turns to dust and blows away? What's underneath isn't so shiny. Like the veins that run beneath our skin, the hopes, dreams, embarrassments, and shames of our life ebb and flow. This is where the ugly resides, and if you based your selection on pieces that fit together too easily, the ugly will be rejected. The second layer needs love, and love is not what it will get. All the love was used up on the luminous outer layer, the external. The perfect. Natalie loved Henry because he was good on paper. A handsome, loyal man who would one day be a good provider. Henry loved Natalie because she was beautiful, kind, and would one day become the stay-at-home mother of his dreams.

Henry didn't know that Natalie hums songs on repeat until a person could drown in their own irritation, or that she keeps a dresser drawer full of dirty laundry she doesn't want to wash. I watched Natalie fall in love with the relationship she had carefully constructed to ensure a better ending than her parents'. Maybe I should've opened my mouth again, let the warning spill out and damn the consequences. It's too late now, though, and Natalie learned the lesson the hard way.

"Are you seeing this?" Rob bumps me with an elbow.

I nod and drain my beer. I'm staring at the giant TV in front of us, watching as the Yankee's ringer steps up to the plate. There's a guy on first and one on third. The one on third edges away from the bag, only to creep back when the pitcher turns and pretends to throw it to his third baseman. Finally, he winds up and throws it to home plate. My heart stops at the crack of the bat, and my breath stays near the top of my throat as the ball sails high, and it goes, goes, goes, until it's somewhere in the stands.

Pushing off my bar stool, I stand and yell, my cheer lost in the sea of celebration. High-fives from strangers feels normal for a minute, and then the excitement dies down until it's only a buzzing in my chest. I pick up my phone to text Natalie, wanting to share the excitement even though I know she doesn't care, but our most recent text conversation distracts me.

When I told her about not taking Allison home that night, I'd wanted Natalie to be happy. I'd wanted her to tell me that, yes, she was disappointed when she saw me.

I'd certainly confused Allison, especially after working so hard to get her to understand why I'd left in the middle of our previous date. After we'd run into Natalie, I couldn't bring Allison's back to my place and do what we'd both thought we'd do that night. I'd faked a migraine, and walked Allison to her building. On my walk home, instead of seeing Allison's confused expression, all I could see was Natalie's shocked face, the emotion swimming in her eyes.

Why not us, Aidan?

Her question is never far from my thoughts, bouncing from brain cell to brain cell. A question like that must've come from somewhere, but the indifferent tone of her messages says otherwise.

My thumb hovers over the screen, in limbo, when three little dots appear. *What? She's writing me?*

The dots disappear and return. Disappear and return. Her message pops up.

Congrats! Your football team won.

Her message is followed by an upside down smiley face.

Smiling at her football reference, I write back and hit send.

Football is my favorite sport.

Natalie: Mine too. So about Thanksgiving...

You're canceling on me?

Natalie: Not exactly. But I talked to my mom and she laid the annual guilt trip on me. Hard.

Hard like concrete or hard like the erection of a man who should admit he needs medicine to get it up?

Natalie: Ewwwww.

Well???

Natalie: Concrete hard. Can we go to her place first and then to your parents'?

Sure. What about your dad?

Natalie: He's coming to the city this year. I'm seeing him the night before. At a Chinese restaurant.

Nothing says Pilgrims and Native Americans like a steaming dish of Lo Mein.

Natalie: I know, right? Pick me up at eleven?

Her assumption that I'm renting a car is accurate. It's one of the few luxuries I allow myself. The winding street on the way to my parents' house is thick with trees on both sides, and a street like that deserves a car hugging its curves. Taking the train out to Pound Ridge feels like an implied insult.

I'll be there. With my driving gloves. No arguments.

Natalie hates my driving gloves. To be honest, I wear them to annoy her. Though it doesn't hurt that my hands are encased in soft fabric while I'm doing it.

She responds only with an eye roll emoji.

I run a finger above my top lip and scroll through tonight's conversation. No mention of what happened a few nights ago. Not even a joke to smooth things over. I could have made a facetious comment like *I haven't talked to you in four years*, to which she would've replied, *Actually it's been five*.

But, no. Nothing. Just a hop into conversation as though nothing disrupted its flow in the first place.

I guess we're just going to act like it never happened.

11

NATALIE

WHY DOES THE SIGHT OF THAT BLONDE-HAIRED, DOE-EYED little snot eating food off the ground give me such pleasure? Surely that's not the right feeling to have? As I watch, his two small fingers reach out, pinching a pea like a crab seizing whatever the hell it is crabs eat.

Allegra, my father's new wife, peeks under the table and spots her precious angel inserting the pea and what I assume are at least three million microscopic bacteria into his mouth.

"No, Jagger. No!" She moves quickly, her chair scraping against the red tile floor. I wince at the sound it makes, but it's a good cover up for the amusement that was surely showing on my face.

Allegra comes up from under the table with Jagger in tow. She sets him back down in his chair and whips out an iPad from her purse. Within seconds Jagger's eyes are wide, the screen putting him in a trance.

"I wish we would've had those when you girls were

small." My father nods at the iPad. "Maybe we would've gone out for dinner more often."

I eye him, trying not to show the disgust that's making my stomach churn. *We didn't go out because people would've wanted to know why Mom wore a sweater in July.*

The words die somewhere in my throat. I don't know if Allegra knows about the abuse. I don't know if Allegra experiences it herself. She's wearing a cowl neck sweater tonight, but of course, it's November. Maybe I should pay them a surprise visit in the summer.

"Yeah, iPads are great," I respond. Instead of paying attention to me, he's looking around the restaurant. First at the shelf on the right, where there is a large porcelain statue of a cat, then around the whole place. It's a small restaurant, so it doesn't take long for him to finally look back at me. In the past year, the gray in his hair has increased ten-fold, and the bags under his eyes have become a permanent fixture. I wonder how often he is mistaken for Jagger's grandfather?

Our conversation, which was paltry at best, ceases completely. The air is thick with discomfort. I have almost nothing to say to the man who raised me. Nothing to say to the man who used his hands to push me on the swings then used those same hands to hurt my mother. A fissure split him in two the first time I noticed a bruise on her arm. I cannot reconcile the two versions of my father, and a small part of me hates him. Not just for what he did to her, but for what he did to me and Sydney. He took away our happy family, an offense so grievous it pours over every good thing he's ever done, leaving nothing but midnight black on memories that should be white.

"So, Henry," my dad starts, pausing to assess what hearing Henry's name will do to me. "How's he doing?"

I shrug. "I don't know. I haven't seen him since the papers were signed."

My dad looks surprised. "You said you were leaving him. I didn't realize it was final."

I nod. "Oh. Hmm." What is my response supposed to be?

"Was he bad to you?" My dad's voice is gruff as he entertains the possibility that perhaps I suffered the same fate as my mother.

I stare at him until he begins to look uncomfortable, then I say, "No, Dad. Not in the way you're referencing."

He has the decency to look embarrassed. Allegra rubs his forearm in a soothing way that pisses me off, and he sends a tight smile in her direction. Maybe she does know about the abuse.

"Henry wasn't good or bad," I say, removing my silverware from its place inside the rolled up paper napkin. I place the napkin on my lap and set out the silverware. "He wasn't the right man for me. I made a mistake when I married him, and the longer the marriage went on, the more apparent that became." I don't feel like airing our dirty laundry. Besides, there is no use telling my father that every day I woke up feeling like I was choking on my own fear. He would never understand such a feeling.

Quiet descends again, punctuated every few seconds by a child's voice from Jagger's iPad. I'm so grateful when the food arrives that I shove a steaming piece of orange chicken between my lips and scald the roof of my mouth. Oddly, the pain is almost worth it.

When dinner is over, my dad pays the check and tells me they'll be staying in the city tonight instead of heading back to their home in Connecticut.

"We have a hotel," he says, and Allegra smiles at him, her eyes shiny with excitement.

She looks at me and explains. "My sister lives in the city, and we're having Thanksgiving dinner with them tomorrow."

"That's nice," I respond, hoping my smile looks genuine.

Allegra's eyes widen and she grabs for my arm. "You can come, of course. My sister would love to meet you."

My arm is still in her grip, and even through all our layers, it feels wrong to be touched by her. Like I'm cheating on my mother. "Thank you for the invite, but I'm going to Pound Ridge with Aidan. His parents' place," I add when I see my father's confusion.

We say goodbye, and I'm the first to turn around. I wait seven seconds, then peek back around. There they go, their backs to me, walking with Jagger between them. My dad holds hands with him and then grins down at something Jagger has said. I frown at the sight, and my orange chicken threatens a reappearance in the world.

They look so happy together, and I wonder if they truly are. Then I wonder why my mother, my sister, and I couldn't make him that happy.

* * *

IT WOULD BE REALLY FUCKING NICE IF MY SISTER WOULD STOP being my sister for two seconds and agree to give me backup at my mom's tomorrow. I've threatened, I've cajoled, I've even promised to find a guy to help her release steam for a night. It all got me nowhere.

"I disown you," I announce to Sydney, cradling the

phone between my shoulder and my ear so I can continue throwing things into a bag.

"Not possible," she responds, crunching on a chip. "Tell me about seeing Dad."

I sigh. I don't really want to talk about seeing my father, but I know she's curious. Due to proximity more than choice, I see him more often than she does.

I recount the story, word for word, and Sydney responds the way she should in all the right places. Until I get to the end, anyhow. She doesn't care about them walking hand in hand, looking picture perfect.

"You have to get over that shit, Natalie. Dad moved on. Mom is basically a lunatic. I say you forget about seeing her tomorrow and just go to Aidan's. He's more family than they'll ever be."

"Yeah..." I say, my voice trailing off. If he's family, then I pulled an incestuous move.

"What?" Dread colors Sydney's question.

"It's nothing." I shake my head even though she can't see me. "It's just that I got really drunk last week and said something stupid and now things are weird between me and Aidan." My gaze falls down to my nearly full bag. "It should make for a great drive tomorrow."

"What did you say?"

Heat colors my cheeks at the thought of my words. I don't really even care that I undressed in front of him. It's not like I did a dance and peacocked around the bathroom before slipping into the tub. And besides, he turned around until I was safely underwater.

"I asked him why we've never gotten together." I cringe, picturing his expression. His mouth had set in a grim line, and that confused me. I don't know what my goal was in asking him that question, but it certainly wasn't to upset him. He should've laughed. Rolled his eyes. Joked about my drunkenness. Why on earth did my question upset him?

Sydney lets out a low whistle. "What did he say?"

"He said *'You know me, Nat. I'm not a commitment guy.'* That was the end of it."

"Well, that was awkward."

"Um hmm." Sitting back on the bed, I push my overnight bag out of the way and cross one ankle over the other.

"Nat?"

"Yeah?"

"Why did you ask him that question? I thought you guys were on the same page about being platonic."

"We are."

She doesn't say anything, and I know she's silent because she's waiting for me to give her more to go on.

I sigh in a deep, annoyed, dramatic way. I don't want to have this conversation because I don't know what to say. *I* don't know why I asked the question, so how the hell am I supposed to explain it to someone else?

"I'm not sure why I asked him that. I really, truly do not know. One minute I was soaking in a bath and the next I was asking him the worst thing ever. And—"

"Wait. Back up. You were in a bath when you asked him?"

Oh. Right. I hadn't mentioned that part before.

"After I threw up on myself, Aidan ran a bath for me. I was light-headed and didn't want to be alone in the bath. He stayed, but turned around until I was safely under bubbles."

"I'd say you crossed a line before you even asked that question."

"Thanks, Sydney. That's helpful."

She laughs at my sarcasm. "I'm just saying, the lines were already blurring. It makes perfect sense why you asked him. You were drunk, vulnerable, and a line in your friendship was already starting to resemble a watercolor."

I like her justification. In fact, I like it so much I'm going to go with it. "That sounds about right," I tell her. "I believe you just won your case, Ms. Maxwell."

She barks a laugh. "Unfortunately, I can't help you with your other problem."

"What's that?" I ask, adjusting the pillows behind me.

"Mom. You're going to have to take one for the team."

"Thanks a lot."

We talk for a few more minutes, then hang up. I climb off the bed and look down at my open overnight bag. There's just enough room for one more thing, but I don't know if I have the guts to do it.

12
NATALIE

DESPITE ALL THE NOISE ON THE CROWDED STREET, I HEAR THE roar of the engine before I see the car. I look down through the busy street crowded with cabs and regular vehicles, my eyes seeking out a small sports car. When Aidan drives out of the city, he always does it in a shiny black Porsche 911 Turbo. He generally denies himself the use of his trust fund but allows himself this one small pleasure.

In the lane closest to me, four cars back sits Aidan and his temporary toy. Traffic is at a standstill, but I can still hear the engine purring. Our eyes meet through the windshield, and Aidan guns the engine. The sound of it reverberates through my chest. Even from this distance, I can see the light in his eyes, the way his fingers grip the steering wheel. The light is red, but it won't be for long. With my heavy bag weighing me down on one side, I hurry down the sidewalk. Aidan gets out and moves to the back of the car, lifting the trunk. When I get there, he takes the bag from my shoulder. I must not have zipped one side all the way, because a few things spill out onto the dirty street.

"Shit," I mutter, bending down to snatch my brick red and ivory striped pajamas from the ground.

The light must've turned green because the car behind us inches forward.

Aidan reaches for my pajamas and stuffs them into the bag. I spy my face cream under the car. My *really expensive* face cream.

"Aidan, I need that!" The stress of the situation causes my voice to rise a few octaves. I point under the car and look up at Aidan. The car behind us honks, and it's not the short sound of a polite honk. No, it's a long, loud blast and it's so goddamn close that it sounds like a foghorn trumpeting right into my ears. Aidan glares at the driver and flips them off. The driver returns the motion and turns on his blinker, trying to move around us. He is still mouthing who knows what as he speeds past us.

"Happy Thanksgiving, asshole," Aidan yells back. He walks to the driver side, opens the door and leans in, and suddenly the hazards are flashing near my head.

Aidan reappears beside me and bends down so we're nearly eye to eye. "Okay, now that that's out-of-the-way, what is it you need so badly? Please don't say it's a tube of lip gloss."

I reach out and pinch his arm. "Of course not. It's only the world's most expensive face cream."

Aidan nods, but his expression is derisive. "Ah, yes. Face cream. An item that can be bought at nearly every street corner in America."

I reach out again to pinch him, but this time he knows it's coming and grabs my wrist mid-air. "I'm kidding."

He drops down onto his knees and peers underneath the car. It's so low to the ground that it can't be easy for him.

After a few seconds, he grips the bumper of the car with his left hand, his right hand disappearing underneath. A moment later he sits up with his arm outstretched, his fingers curled around my precious bottle of youth in a jar.

"Thank you," I tell him, resisting the urge to wrap my arms around him. We both stand, and I tuck the bottle back into my bag and double check that it's zipped properly.

"You're welcome." He slams the trunk closed and glances at me. "Please don't lose it in the garbage. I'm not a big fan of dumpster diving."

Laughing, I walk around to the passenger side and open the door. I have to bend my knees to slide into the low profile car. The light has gone through a full cycle and is red again, but just like before, I know it won't be red for long.

"Not too shabby," I say when Aidan gets in and closes his door. My fingers slip over the supple leather seats.

"It's a 2018," Aidan grins. "I lucked out. They just happened to have this model available."

From the center compartment, he produces his black driving gloves. It's not until this moment that I realized he didn't have them on during the face cream fiasco. He makes a show of putting them on, trying to entice me to comment. I say nothing, looking out at the street.

"You should probably start to drive unless you were looking to get into another verbal altercation," I say, pointing up at the now green light.

Aidan taps on the gas pedal and the car flies forward, sending me slamming back into my seat.

Aidan looks at me sheepishly. "It takes a little getting used to."

I nod my head, my lower lip captured between my teeth to keep from laughing.

I spent a lot of last night stressing over what this car ride would be like. Needless to say, I did not anticipate making a spectacle of ourselves in the middle of a crowded Manhattan Street. It was just what we needed to break the awkwardness that's been sitting between us.

"How was your week?" It seems like an innocuous enough question, and a good way to start conversation.

Aidan runs a hand through his unkempt hair and shifts gears. He seems to be considering my question, and then he answers. "I guess it was okay. None of those little shits wanted to do any work this week. They came into my classroom already on vacation."

"To be honest, I'm pretty sure I went into work already on vacation this week."

"If I was in your line of work, I'd want to be on a permanent vacation."

I roll my eyes. Aidan and accountant really doesn't mix. Then again, I never thought Aidan and math teacher mixed either, and yet somehow they do. Maybe it's because Aidan doesn't look like a traditional math teacher. Even in his work clothes, which consist of jeans and a button-down shirt, there's something about him, some underlying wildness. Like even though his wildness can be tempered, it can't be tamed.

"I could definitely do your job," I say confidently, crossing my arms in front of myself.

"I have no doubt that you could." Aidan looks over at me. "The question is, do you want another number job?"

I think about my manuscript. At this very minute, it's tucked away in my bag, down at the very bottom. Maybe if the opportunity arises, I'll show it to Aidan's mom. *Maybe*. Even five minutes of her time would be worth its weight in gold. I hate the idea of taking advantage of my connection, but I know it's foolish not to.

I reach forward, pushing buttons until the radio comes on. Then I push more buttons until I find something suitable to listen to. "You know what kind of job I want, Aidan."

Aidan makes a fist and shakes it in front of him. "Take it. Make it yours," he says in a rough voice. I'm almost positive he's quoting one of those war movies he likes so much.

"I saw your manuscript in your bag, Nat."

"Forget you saw it, Aidan. I brought it so I can work on it if I have downtime."

"It's finished."

"There are always little things I can tweak."

He holds up one hand and mouths the word '*fine.*'

We settle into the drive as Aidan moves farther out of the city. The streets are quieter than I thought they would be for a holiday. Probably because people usually travel the day before, not on the actual holiday. I change stations again and find Christmas music, and then I leave it there. Some people don't believe in Christmas music till after Thanksgiving, but I am firmly not one of those people. I've even been known to listen to Christmas music in July.

I'm humming along to my fifth Christmas song when Aidan does it. The dreaded nose pick. We're just about to get on the I-95 and are waiting at a red light. He removed his gloves a few minutes ago, probably because they were getting hot, and now his fingers are free to roam.

"Are you finding anything good in there?" I can't help myself. Not pointing it out might kill me.

Aidan withdraws his finger from his nose and gives me a dirty look. "I had to do something with my hands to keep them from reaching over and quieting your humming."

For clarification, he places a cupped hand over his own mouth.

In the past, his comment wouldn't have bothered me. But for some reason right now, sitting in this car, trying as hard as we can not to think about what I said and let it affect us, his comment sets a flush to my cheeks. Something has shifted between us and I feel vulnerable.

"I'm sorry, I didn't realize my humming was so annoying." My hands go between my knees and I press them together.

"Hey," Aidan says softly. I look up at him. His eyes are crinkled in concern.

"I don't care if you hum. I'm sorry. I didn't mean to hurt your feelings." He has to look away from me to drive, but because I don't have to move my eyes anywhere, I keep them on his profile. There's an uneasy feeling in my stomach, and I don't like it. When did this happen to us? Are we really so weak that just a few words could put us in this place, dancing this awkward dance? Were we really only as strong as our resolve to not let this become something else?

Aidan stares ahead, keeping his eyes on the traffic as he joins the other cars on the I-95. I've looked at his face a thousand times before, but suddenly I'm seeing him through a different lens. Inside me is a yearning, almost an ache. I want to reach out and run my fingertips over his stubble, push his hair back from his eyes. His posture is relaxed, but the hand that's not on the steering wheel drums a beat with his fingers on his knee. I want to reach out and steady his hand, ask him what he's thinking. Is he feeling what I'm feeling? Impending doom? Anticipating loss?

Suddenly Aidan's eyes are on mine, and because I was so lost in my feelings, I didn't look away quickly enough. There is trepidation in those brown eyes. Behind the caramel flecks, I see his worry. He feels it too, this tight rope we're balancing on.

I haven't been paying attention to the music, but apparently Aidan has. He looks away from me and touches a button on the steering wheel. The beginning of "Baby It's Cold Outside" fills the small car.

"But baby it's cold outside," Aidan sings softly, glancing at me with upraised eyebrows.

I watch him for a moment. He tilts his head forward, encouraging me to pick up the female's lines.

A smile curves my lips despite the sick feeling still sitting in my stomach. "This evening has been," I sing.

"Been hoping that you drop in." Aidan makes his voice even deeper on purpose.

The longer we sing, the more the feeling in the pit of my stomach melts away.

I point my finger at him and sing, "I ought to say no, no, no sir."

"Mind if I move in closer?" Aidan leans his forearm on the center console and pushes his shoulder against mine.

It's only a stupid song lyric, but I can't help the way my heart beats double time.

Aidan's face is just inches from mine. Our eyes meet, and he straightens up. The next few lines of the song go unsung. Aidan uses that same button on the steering wheel to turn down the volume.

"You can hum the rest of the drive, Natalie. I promise I don't care."

"You can pick your nose, if you want to. I mean, you don't do it egregiously. It's just, like, the tip of your finger is in there. Like this." I demonstrate it for him, and he laughs. "Like maybe you just have an itch or something."

Aidan waves his hand. "Okay, enough talking about me doing something reserved for grandpas sitting in recliners all day."

"Don't be embarrassed, Aidan. Everybody picks their nose."

"Even you?" Aidan raises one eyebrow at me and smirks.

"Yep." I grin at him. This feels normal. This feels like the old Aidan and Natalie before I adopted an alcohol-soluble filter.

"How did it go seeing your dad last night?"

I can't help but make a face. "How do you think it went?"

"Not great, I'm assuming?"

"Jagger ate off the floor. That was pretty much the high point of the evening."

Aidan barks a laugh.

"I can't figure out my dad and Allegra."

"Maybe you aren't meant to."

My lips twist as I mull his comment over. Maybe Aidan is right. Maybe I am not meant to understand my dad and Allegra. Maybe what it is, just...is.

"Want to take bets on how deep my mom is by the time we arrive?"

Aidan rubs a hand over the stubble on his left cheek. "Hmm. I'm going to say just one. He glances at the clock on the dash. "It's still early in the day, and she's probably excited that we're coming. I don't think she'll be sloshed yet."

Perhaps Aidan needs reminding of who it is we're talking about. My mother can drink a sailor on leave under the table. Among other things, it's a skill she has acquired since she and my dad divorced.

I decide to skip the reminder, mostly because Aidan doesn't need one. "I'm going to say she'll be two drinks in by the time we arrive. At least," I add, just to make sure Aidan knows I don't agree with his guesstimation.

And guess what? I'm right. I know it within five seconds of my mother opening her door. One drink would've definitely gotten a smile. But two drinks? Two drinks gets us an *I'm so happy to see you*. My mother is never *so happy* to do anything. She basically hates life until given alcohol. At least she is a happy drunk. It could be worse.

She hugs me first, then Aidan.

I can feel her muscles underneath her blouse. Besides drinking, there's another thing my mother picked up: weights. More specifically, going to the gym for two hours every day.

"Aidan, what is that cologne? It smells delightful." My mother pulls away from Aidan, running an appraising look over him.

We've only just gotten here and already I want to sink down into the ground.

"Thanks, Annette. Eau de Aidan," he jokes.

My mother turns, leaving the door wide open and walking to the rest of the house. We follow and I hear her say, "Natalie I don't know why you haven't snapped him up yet." She holds her hands out to the side and makes snapping sounds. I glance at Aidan and roll my eyes. He shrugs and gives me a look of as if to say *well what are you gonna do*? We follow her to the kitchen at the back of the house. A bottle of red wine sits on the counter, and it's half gone. Surreptitiously I point at it. Aidan's eyes follow to where I'm pointing, and he looks back at me. I hold up two fingers, mouthing the words "I win," and do a tiny jig behind my mom's back.

Mom reaches into the cabinet and pulls out two more glasses. She divides the contents of the bottle into those two glasses and hands them to us. I hadn't planned on drinking this early, and I still don't, but I take it from her anyway. It's easier to take it and dump it slowly over the course of my time here than it is to argue with her about why I'm not drinking.

"Dinner will be ready in twenty minutes," my mother announces after she clinks glasses with ours. I look over at the oven and it's not on. Neither is the microwave. Or the toaster oven. I turn confused eyes to my mother.

She brings a cupped hand to her mouth and giggles. "I ordered take-out!" She looks so proud of herself that I offer her a high-five. She slaps my hand and says, "Did you know there is an app where you can order from almost any restaurant you want, and somebody will deliver it to you?"

I smile at her exuberance. "Yep. What did you order for today?"

"Lasagna!" Mom claps her hands together. "I thought it would be a fun departure from the typical turkey and mashed potatoes."

"It sure is," I tell her, smiling. Last night I ate dinner in China. Today, I'll have lunch in Italy. At least I know that tonight I will be firmly in America.

"Come on." Mom motions with her hands. She pushes off from the counter and walks away, and we follow her to the living room. "Let's sit here and enjoy our wine while we wait for our food."

Mom settles into a floral upholstered chair, and Aidan

and I are on the small sofa across from her. This is my mother's home, but it's basically foreign to me. She moved here after the divorce. I was already in college, so I never lived here. My sister lived here for one year before she fled for the nation's capital, but something tells me even she would say this home is foreign to her. Our childhood home is seven miles from here, and I haven't been back since the day I moved out. My mother boxed up everything I left behind when I went to college and brought them here. I spent eight hours one Saturday going through everything, and what I chose to keep now sits in her office closet. One day when I'm finally settled somewhere, I'll take it all with me. I just don't know when that day will be.

I'm focusing on an oil painting of flowers that hangs on the wall when Mom says, "So, Aidan, how's work? You're a math teacher, right? Bet you have all those high school girls batting their eyelashes at you." She tries to sound nonchalant, but something in her tone makes me feel uncomfortable. And if I'm uncomfortable, then Aidan must be too.

His nervous chuckle tells me my assumption is correct. Rubbing his palms on his jean-covered thighs, he says, "Well, not too much. I do my best to politely ignore them. Even accidental encouragement, no matter how small, can get out of hand. Teenage hormones, you know?"

Mom makes a sound like a laugh, but the sound stays stuck in her throat, so it sounds more like *mmmm*. "I remember those hormones. Don't you?" She looks at me with her eyebrows raised.

"I suppose." *Why are we talking about this?* "Are you dating anybody, Mom?" As soon as the words are out of my mouth, I realize how stupid they are. Last I checked, my mom hates men. The marks left on her by my father's hand have stayed long after they've healed.

Mom blinks and looks away. "No. Nobody has managed to catch my eye yet." She's gazing out the front window. I turn wide eyes to Aidan and mouth the word *help.*

"Annette, my mom still has a lot of contacts in this town. Would you mind if I asked her if she knows of any eligible bachelors?"

Mom shifts her gaze back to Aidan. Her eyes are guarded now. Gone is her light and airy flirtatiousness. Bad memories have slipped in and taken the reins.

She gives Aidan a small smile. "That's sweet of you Aidan, but I'll have to decline your offer. Nobody wants someone with this much baggage." Both hands reach down and grasp the air, as though she is picking up two suitcases. She lifts the pretend suitcases a few inches into the air and drops them.

"Mom—" I start, but she interrupts me.

"Natalie, it's okay. I'm okay." She peers past me, out the front window again, but this time she stands. "The food is here."

Aidan stands also and follows my mom to the front door. He takes the food from the delivery man, and my mom frets over the fact that the deliveryman is working on Thanksgiving. "You should come in and eat with us," she says.

I walk over and join Aidan and my mom at the front door.

"It's fine, really." The guy backs up a few feet. With his acne dotted skin and hair that hangs unevenly over his ears, he's really more of a teenage boy than a man. "I get paid double time on holidays."

This appeases my mother, and she lets the delivery boy go. Closing the door, she shrugs and says, "I tried."

Despite my irritation at my mother, a surge of love for her flows over me. Wrapping one arm around her shoulders, I squeeze her and tell her, "You can't take care of everybody."

We go to the kitchen, where Aidan and I open containers while my mother removes plates from the cabinet above the toaster oven.

I suck in a quick shocked breath when I see the plates she has set out. "Mom, are you sure?"

Mom nods once, slowly. "I don't know why I kept them." She traces the design on her wedding china with a fingertip. "Seems silly, doesn't it?"

"No, Mom. No, it doesn't."

Mom reaches over and pulls a serving spoon from a drawer. She hands it to Aidan, and he takes care of portioning out the lasagna.

Mom opens a new bottle of wine and pours herself a glass. She takes one look at my nearly full glass but doesn't say anything. Instead she says, "Did you keep anything from Henry?"

"Honestly, I'm not sure. I packed pretty quickly. I'm sure there are some things of his in my boxes. I haven't been through them all yet." I had unpacked all the things I thought I would need. There were three boxes left over, and those were pushed to the bottom of my closet. It only makes sense that there are relics of Henry buried somewhere in there.

Aidan, who has been quiet this whole time, speaks up. "His letterman jacket." Aidan brings his gaze to mine, the serving spoon dangling from his right hand. "I packed

Henry's letterman jacket. I didn't even realize it until right now." Aidan shakes his head. "He's probably going to want that back."

"Don't worry about it," I assure him. He looks annoyed with himself. "It's not like I can avoid him forever."

"You had a better chance of it before I packed something of his in your box." He sighs and picks up two plates, holding them out to me and my mom.

I set my plate down on the counter and step closer to Aidan. "I'm not upset. You shouldn't be either." My hand goes to his upper arm and I give it a squeeze. Aidan looks down at me.

Those eyes, the ones that have always brought me such safety and security, look troubled. "It upsets you to see him."

I can't deny his words, because they're true. But I'm surprised to see Aidan reacting this way. It's out of character for him.

Stepping back, I grab our plates from the countertop and turn, motioning with my head to the small table in the dining room. "Let's eat while it's still hot."

We eat in silence, and neither Aidan or I touch our wine. My mom finishes her third glass and pours a fourth. I could ask her to stop, but what the fuck is the point? If I was in her position, I might want four glasses of wine too.

After we finish, Aidan steps out to call his mom while I wash our three dinner plates and mine and Aidan's wine glasses. Mom leans on the countertop beside me.

"Have you seen your father?"

"Last night," I respond without looking at her. Running water pours over my finger as I wait for it to be hot enough. When it is, I grab the dish soap and pour it onto a scrub brush.

"How is he?" she asks.

Does she really want to know? Am I supposed to tell her that he seems really fucking happy with his new family? *Happy Thanksgiving, Mom, I came here to eat lasagna and hurt your feelings.*

"His kid ate food off the floor of a Chinese restaurant that I'm certain wouldn't pass health inspection." I look up from my scrubbing and catch her laughing.

"I shouldn't laugh at that," she says, pulling away the hand she'd used to cover her laughter.

"Yes, you should. It's funny." I hand her a washed and rinsed plate and she picks up a towel to dry it.

"And his wife?" That last word holds so much pain for her. *Wife.* A figurative slap in the face.

"She seems happy. I don't know for sure, but I think he's getting help. Or has already gotten it. I don't know." The way Allegra soothed my dad last night after my comment made me think maybe he has sought help.

Mom takes the next plate I have held out but doesn't meet my eyes. I look harder and see the shiny tears she is holding back.

"Good," she says after a few moments. Her voice is shaky but strong. "I don't know Allegra, but she doesn't deserve that. No woman does."

"Of course not," I murmur, pressing down a little harder with a scrub brush on the last plate. If my mom wasn't on her fourth glass of wine, would she be so sanguine about this? She met a man and fell in love, she had his children and experienced pain from his hand, and now someone else will get the best of him. If that isn't fucked up, then I don't know what it is. Nobody ever said life has to be easy, but does it have to be so damn hard?

"Do you miss Henry?" My mother takes the final plate from me and dries it off. I wish I had something to do with my hands, but there are no more dishes. Gathering my long hair, I pull it over one shoulder and divide it into three sections to make a braid.

"No," I say slowly, thinking about my answer. Perhaps I should miss him more, but I don't. Maybe it's because we weren't married for very long. Maybe it's because I'd fallen out of love with him long before I signed the divorce papers. Or maybe it's because I've always had Aidan for companionship, love, and understanding.

"Do you think that's because you have Aidan?"

For a moment I wonder whether I just spoke my thoughts aloud. Knowing that I did not, I open my mouth to answer my mom's question.

"Probably. Having Aidan as my best friend gives me everything I would have in a partner. Minus the sex, obviously." This is a good reminder that I should never say anything like I did that night in the bathtub. I need Aidan too much to risk him. Any thoughts like that should stay on the inside of my head.

"I wonder if you and Aidan could ever be more." Mom tips up her glass and drinks but keeps her eyes on me.

I shake my head. "No, Mom. We know better. There is a line and we do not cross it."

My mother eyes me. "You never know. I wonder how you'd feel if push ever comes to shove."

"What do you mean?"

"One day you'll meet someone. Or one day, he'll meet someone. And then what?"

Aidan's blonde, fairylike date springs to mind. We haven't spoken of her since the night I saw them together.

"We've already been through that once, remember? Everything worked out fine."

"Did it though? Have you ever asked him how he felt watching you get married?"

"I've never had a reason to." Now her question has me mentally sifting through my memories of that time period. Closer to the beginning of my relationship with Henry, Aidan came to me and told me his doubts. I didn't listen. I was in love and overwhelmed by Henry. It's not lost on me that the parts of his personality that I fell in love with were the same traits that slowly suffocated me. I met Henry not long after my parents' divorce was finalized, and I needed what he had to offer. I needed to be led by someone who seemed like they knew what they were doing. Grasping for proof that not all men were like my father, I'd latched on to Henry. He was confident and secure, and just so capable. Able to accomplish anything. Able to talk anybody into anything. I'd grown up waiting for the day when I would fall in love, and then I watched my parents and was hit with the stark reality of what love can turn into. I was ripe for love that didn't hurt, and Henry was right there to give it.

Aidan was by my side through all of that. One time he tried to intervene. My response had ensured it would be the only time. I didn't want to hear the truth, and after Aidan offered it up, he stepped back and stayed tight-lipped. He hugged me after I got engaged, and stood with me at the altar. Did I ever ask how it made him feel to see me get married? No. I did not ask him for his thoughts, and he did not share his opinions. If I had put down the wedding planning magazine, if I had closed Pinterest and looked at Aidan, would I have seen an objection that wanted to come out? Maybe the objection hung there in the air, like a child with his hand raised in a classroom full of students, just waiting to be called upon. Maybe I didn't look too hard, because I didn't want to see it. I thought Henry was my chance at the perfect love my parents did not have. And I thought wrong. I could call myself silly and young, naïve. But at the bottom of it all, it's plain and simple. I was wrong. And Aidan knew it.

I open my mouth, planning on telling my mom that she can get rid of any romantic notions about me and Aidan, but the back door opens and Aidan walks in. His cheeks are red from the cold, and he sniffs, running the back of his hand under his nose.

"Why aren't you wearing your jacket?" I ask.

"I left everything in the car."

"Is your mom okay?"

"She's upset. She dropped the pumpkin pie on the ground." Aidan chuckles. "Apparently my dad came up from behind and tickled her while she was carrying it."

Swoon. I look at my mom. The dreamy look on her face tells me she's thinking the same thing.

"Diego and Diana are relationship goals," my mom says. I can't help my laugh. My mom should take a break from social media.

I nod. "Seriously."

Aidan's mouth draws into a hard line. He doesn't say anything about his parents, and the air around him grows tense. He does this sometimes, and I can't figure out why. I've asked, and he's given me a bullshit answer about how his parents' great love story gets old sometimes. I've never pushed to know the real reason, but I'm still curious.

"I told her we'd pick up a pie on the way over." He looks apologetically at my mother. "We should probably get going. I called a grocery store that's on the way and they are closing in thirty minutes."

"Of course, of course. I understand." Mom reaches out with her free hand and sets it on Aidan's shoulder. "Thanks for bringing my girl out to see me."

"We wouldn't miss it, Annette." Aidan brushes a quick kiss on her cheek.

Mom pats the spot where he kissed. "You're going to make this old lady blush."

Oh Lord.

"Well, we'd better go," I say, kicking into gear and grabbing my bag from the counter. I wind it over my arm and hug my mom.

"Thank you for today, Mom. It was good to see you." She winds her arms around me, and guilt hits me right in the stomach as I inhale her familiar scent. From now on, I'm going to make more of an effort to come up here and visit her. And I'm going to force Sydney to come too.

We leave, the door swinging closed behind us. Aidan rubs his palms together and then blows into them.

"Brrr," he says, shaking his shoulders to emphasize the word.

"What happened back there?" We climb into the rental car and quickly close the doors. It's at least forty degrees outside.

"What are you talking about?" Aidan starts the car and puts it into drive.

"You. Getting tense about my mom and I swooning over your dad's awesomeness. Do you really hate relationships that much that you can't handle us swooning over your parents?"

"No, Natalie. I do not hate relationships."

"Could've fooled me," I grumble, my upper lip lifting on one side.

"Are you snarling?" Aidan looks at me with tight lips, like he's trying not to laugh.

My own lips rearrange into a smile. "Not on purpose."

Aidan reaches over and lightly tugs my bottom lip. "Maybe I should call you raccoon. Some kind of small fierce animal." He takes his finger away from my lip and snaps his fingers. "Honey badger! That's what you are."

"I prefer if you just call me Best."

"Boring," Aidan draws out the word as he says it. "Honey badger is definitely better."

"If you ever call me honey badger, I will bludgeon you."

For the rest of the drive to the grocery store, we argue about his new nickname for me. I know what he is doing, and I also know that I'm letting him do it. He doesn't want to talk about whatever it is that upset him, and I don't have the heart to force him. For right now, in this moment, we are just us again.

13

AIDAN

I feel like an ass.

I stood there in the kitchen, both women overcome with the idea of my dad's romantic gesture, and I couldn't keep it together. I don't hate love. What I hate are lies.

The store has plenty of pumpkin pie, but my mom will still be upset. It wasn't just a pumpkin pie. It was her special maple pumpkin pie with cinnamon graham cracker crust. I don't remember a Thanksgiving that didn't have that pie. I also don't remember Thanksgiving where I didn't get up in the middle of the night and sneak downstairs to have a slice. Grabbing a basic pumpkin pie off the top of the stack, I make my way to the cashier and then out to the car where Natalie sits, waiting for me. I left it running with her inside so she would stay nice and warm.

"Here." I hand her the pie.

"Last one?" Natalie takes it from me and holds it in her lap.

"Yeah, last one," I say sarcastically. "We almost had Thanksgiving without pumpkin pie." I look over at Natalie.

Her eyes haven't stopped being curious since the moment I walked back into her mother's house after the phone call.

Some might say best friends tell each other everything. To me, there are times when not knowing is a gift.

Natalie lifts the pie and examines it. "Meet you in the kitchen tonight at two a.m.?"

"Of course," I say, turning onto the road that will lead us to my parents. I reach over and yank on Natalie's seatbelt. "Just making sure," I tell her. She gives me a knowing look and grips the pie.

With just the slightest amount of pressure on the gas pedal, the car lurches forward. Fallen leaves swirl into the air as we pass, and the nearly bare trees begin to blur. Natalie's eyes are squeezed shut, but she squeals and laughs. She loves the thrill as much as I do.

I slow down before I make the final turn on to my parents' property. My mother will chew me out if she sees me driving that fast. Sneaking a peek at Natalie, I see her chest rise and fall with a deep inhale and exhale. She looks at me and grins.

"That was fun," she says, her voice a little breathless, her eyes dilated.

I wink at her and nod, the car slowly creeping up my parents' long driveway. We wind around some trees and the house comes into view. Parked out front is my father's black Range Rover, and a white SUV I've never seen before.

"Your parents repainted," Natalie murmurs, peering out the windshield.

Their home, previously painted a light tan, is now a colonial blue. The trim is white, and the door is dark gray. My mom spent ten minutes on the phone with me raving about the door she had found. The wreath hanging from the front is a collection of silver metal that has been bent to look like a giant flower. My mom calls it her only perennial flower. I can see why she loves it so much. Right now, all the living things in her yard have gone dormant.

I bring the car to a stop and put it in park. Natalie bends down, grabbing her purse and lifting it up to her shoulder. She reaches for the door handle, then pauses and turns back to me.

"Who is going to be here today? I didn't even think about there being other people since your parents are having it out here."

Natalie's fingers run through her hair and she flips down the visor and looks at herself in the mirror.

"It's my parents, and I think they've invited the neighbors from two houses down." My mom called earlier this week to remind me that I'm supposed to be coming to our house, as if I could possibly forget. Being a schoolteacher means I'm always well aware of all holidays. Plus, I have Natalie to keep me on track.

"What about Shawn?"

"Yes, of course." I can't remember celebrating a single holiday without my father's personal trainer and best friend. When I was younger, I referred to him as my uncle.

"Let's go." I climb from the car and go around to the trunk to unload our bags. Natalie leads the way to the front door. She is wearing her tight jeans, the ones with strategically placed rips in them. It's hard to admit, even to myself, how much I like how she looks in them.

My hands are full with both of our bags, so Natalie opens the door and holds it for me. The house smells like cinnamon and turkey. Laughter filters in from the kitchen at the back of the house. Off to the right is the staircase that leads to the bedrooms where we will be staying. I pause there to drop off our bags, then we move on to the kitchen.

"Aidan!" my mother says when she catches sight of us. She wipes her hands on the bottom corner of her apron and pulls me into a tight hug. She steps back and does the same to Natalie. In a lower voice, I hear her tell Natalie that she looks lovely. Natalie grins and ducks her chin, tucking the hair on the right side of her head behind her ear.

My dad is only a few paces behind my mom. "My son," he exclaims, his excitement thickening his accent. He holds my face in his hands and scrunches one eye, pretending to examine me. "You look good," he declares and hugs me. He moves on to Natalie, who smiles and opens her arms. "You must be the reason he looks so good," he says, stepping into Natalie's arms.

Natalie's eyes flicker to me. For half a second she looks taken aback, then she recovers and says, "Diego, stop. You're making me blush, but fine. I'll take the credit."

My father laughs and steps away, turning and gesturing to the breakfast table. I hadn't noticed three people sitting there.

He gestures to the man first, and then the woman. "This is John and Melinda, they live next door. And this..." He walks quickly to stand behind the third person's chair. "This is Anna."

Anna smiles at me. Her very blonde hair is curled and hangs around her face. I'm not sure how old she is, but I'm guessing she's young. She still has baby fat in her cheeks. Her blue eyes widen as she gets up and walks over to where I'm standing.

"Hi," she says, her smile softening. Beside me, Natalie starts digging through her purse. I'm almost positive she's looking for absolutely nothing, she's just trying to look anywhere but at the preening girl in front of her.

Extending her hand, she says, "I'm Anna. But I guess your father already said that."

Shaking her hand, I say, "Nice to meet you, Anna. I'm Aidan. This is Natalie." Gently I elbow Natalie's side and she looks up.

She smiles apologetically at Anna. "Hi. I'd shake your hand, but I can't give up the search for my lip gloss." Natalie laughs and Anna does too.

I stare at them, confused. Was that some kind of girl secret message?

Anna continues to smile, Natalie continues to fake dig. The atmosphere is turning awkward really fast, so I do the only thing I can think to do. I turn my attention to John and Melinda. I offer them a hand, in turn, tell them it's nice to meet them, and then pepper them with questions I don't care about the answers to.

Anna comes back to her chair at the table and now she's sitting opposite from me. Natalie has apparently given up her search, and now she's beside my mother at the kitchen counter, stirring something in a copper pot on the stove.

Anna is talking about her class load at NYU, but I'm only half listening. My mother and Natalie are talking, and I'm straining to hear their conversation. I don't know why I'm so interested, just that I am.

"...thought Shawn was going to be here," Natalie says.

My mom responds, but I can't hear because her back is turned to me.

Natalie leans in closer to my mom and says something in a hushed tone. Her eyes flicker over to me, and when she sees me watching her, she quickly looks away.

"Aidan, your dad says you're a teacher in the city. What's America's youth like these days?" John's question brings me firmly back into the conversation at the table.

I tell him my funny stories. The ones about the jock and his girlfriend who can't keep their hands off each other, the ones about the best excuses I've ever heard for being late or not having completed homework. I don't tell him about the student in my seventh period class who I'm almost certain is throwing up her lunch, or the kid with holes in the bottoms of his shoes. Telling strangers about those kids' hardships feels like a betrayal.

John rests an arm across the back of Melinda's chair. "Not so different from us then." His smile is a tad smug and it irritates me.

I shake my head in agreement and say nothing. America's youth, as he put it, will never know life without a smartphone, never have to wait through TV commercials, and will probably have a better work-life balance than his generation ever dreamed of having. But sure, they're totally similar.

My dad walks back into the kitchen with a tray balancing four red martinis. Shawn is behind him with a tray of four more. "Who is ready for a cocktail before the meal?"

My hand flies into the air. Out of the corner of my eye, I see Natalie do the same.

My dad serves my mom first, pretending as though he needs a kiss on the cheek before he can give her the drink. She laughs and obliges, and while Melinda and Anna are *aww-ing* about it, I watch Natalie. I've always known the heart can yearn for something, but until this moment I never knew you could watch the feeling on someone's face. Her features have softened, and her eyes are wistful.

I've never understood Natalie's obsession with love. Is she not frightened by the power love wields? Twenty years ago my mom wrote a story about love, and she still gets letters about how it has changed people's lives and convinced them that love is worth the risk. It is only the written word, and it holds power. What would the real thing be like?

Glass clinks on the tabletop as Shawn places a martini in front of me. I look up to thank him and offer him a handshake. Shawn grabs my hand in his and claps me on the back. I cough and lean forward as though he is hurting me, but it's not that far from the truth. Years of personal training have ensured that Shawn is basically like a brick.

"Maybe we ought to get you back in the gym. Toughen you up a bit." He delivers a light one-two punch in my arm.

Shawn is tall, with broad shoulders and perfect, white teeth. His muscles are long and lean. I've never seen him in anything but tiptop shape.

"No way. I'm not going back to the gym with you. You're a maniac."

Shawn raises his glass, and everybody follows suit. "To maniacs."

I meet Natalie's gaze. "To maniacs," we repeat, our eyes on each other, both of us laughing after we say it. Natalie lifts her glass an inch higher, a second toast meant only for me. I mimic her and wink, then toss back the drink. It tastes of cranberry and orange, and it's strong. The drink is chilled, but instantly my chest feels a few degrees warmer.

Natalie puckers her lips after a small sip. "That," she says, setting it down and pointing at the glass, "is trouble."

"That," Anna says, doing the same as Natalie, "is delicious."

My mother announces that dinner will be ready in five minutes, and I take that time to take our bags upstairs. Natalie follows, stopping at the foot of the bed where she'll be sleeping. She reaches for her bag and unzips it.

"Anna seems nice." Natalie removes items from her bag as she speaks.

I shrug. "Yeah, I guess."

Natalie gives me an exasperated look. "Don't tell me you don't know what's going on here."

Her question confuses me. "Apparently you know something I don't. Care to share your knowledge?"

Natalie rolls her eyes and shakes her head. "How can you be so thick?" She removes a pair of black leggings from her bag and sets them on the bed.

Patting my stomach, I say, "I mean, maybe I should take Shawn up on his offer. I could learn to like the gym."

Natalie pulls out her toiletry bag and walks into the adjoining bathroom. Peering into the mirror, she rubs a fingertip under each eye, and says, "They're trying to set you up with Anna."

Oh. I guess I am thick.

Natalie looks at me through the mirror and laughs. "Poor Aidan. You had no idea. Not that it matters. Aren't you seeing Allison?"

I'm not only surprised about this, I'm irritated. "It's pretty bold to set me up with someone when I'm bringing a girl with me." Allison doesn't even factor in. I called her two days ago and told her we were finished. It wasn't a particularly pleasant phone call, but after I ended our last date with a fake migraine, I knew it was over. Our arrangement was casual, and Allison knew that, but when she responded with *You know what Aidan? Go fuck yourself* I realized perhaps things weren't as casual for her.

Natalie straightens and turns, resting the heels of her palms on the countertop behind her. Her gaze is bold and strong. "I'm sure they prepped Anna beforehand. She was expecting you to walk in with me, but she knew I wasn't a threat to her."

Aren't you?

The question tumbles through my body, shocking my brain, immobilizing my tongue and confusing my heart.

I can see my reflection in the mirror. I'm slack-jawed and my eyes are wide, and there is not a thing I can do about it. I am stunned.

Natalie's head tips to the side and her eyes become worried. "Aidan are you—"

"Dinner!" My mother's voice carries upstairs. It's a shame she didn't have more kids, she has the projection to yell for many more people.

"Let's go," I say hastily, spinning around and hurrying through the bedroom. My bag still sits on Natalie's bed, but I can deal with that later. For now, I just need to get out of here. Natalie's four steps behind me the entire way to the table, and I can't imagine what she must be thinking.

"Aidan, sit here." My father motions to a seat. Big surprise that it's right next to Anna. Natalie takes a seat between Shawn and my father. John and Melinda are across from us, and my mom is on Melinda's left. The whole seating arrangement feels very manufactured, and it makes me prickly. As untraditional as it was at Natalie's mom's house, I'm starting to wish we were still there.

Thankfully, the conversation at dinner isn't as on the

nose as the seating arrangement. Melinda asks Shawn a ton of questions about personal training and owning a gym. The group is small enough that it would be difficult to have a side conversation, so we all listen. Twice Anna bumps my foot underneath the table and apologizes. The second time, she adds a giggle to the apology. I wonder if Natalie finds this amusing or irritating? Maybe she hasn't even noticed.

Why do I even care?

Fuck fuck fuck.

I'm confused.

Twenty minutes later, dinner is over. It never fails to amaze me that a meal that takes so long to prepare can be finished so quickly.

"Thank you, Mom." I stand and toss my linen napkin down on the table beside my empty plate.

"You're welcome, dear." Mom smiles at me from across the table. "If you're going to get the pie, I think we should wait awhile. Maybe give it a little time between dinner and dessert."

I couldn't stuff a bite of pie into my mouth if I were being forced, but I don't say that. "I'm going to get a little fresh air. Excuse me," I say to the group, dropping a kiss on the top of my mom's head before I leave the room. Through the kitchen and down a hallway are the doors that lead to the backyard. Once I'm through them, I take a deep, long breath of air that is so crisp I can taste it. The scent of damp earth fills my nose. Shoving my hands in my pockets, I walk down four steps and onto the lawn. Dead leaves crunch under my boots as I head for the tree line.

I need to clear my head, and sitting in that dining room was making me feel like a zoo animal in an exhibit.

I walk fifteen yards into the forest, pausing to lean on the trunk of a tree. Glancing back, I make sure I can see the house from where I am. Getting lost out here would only make things worse. I'm lost enough as it is. These errant, wayward thoughts about Natalie are making me lose my senses. Sighing, I turn back around and face what feels like an endless amount of skinny, barren trees. My eyes close, a deep breath fills my chest, and I allow my thoughts to wander like I never have before. I thought of her in high school, before I got to know her. Back then, those thoughts were mostly pure. Would she finally notice me in history class? Would she accidentally bump into me in the hall? If she did, when she turned to look at me, would her eyes ever hold recognition and longing?

My thoughts now are very different from my thoughts back then. Lifting my hand, I pinch the bridge of my nose and scrunch my already closed eyes.

I've always found Natalie attractive. I'd be lying if I said my eyes never traveled into the front of her shirt if it billowed while she was bending over. These glances were fleeting and never solidified into any concrete thoughts.

But now? My mind doesn't need her to be here for me to bring up the images. Specifically the one from her bathroom the night she got drunk.

Hips gently curving, sliding away into her backside. Dark hair tumbling down to the center of her back. The delicate way she lifted one foot, then the other, and slid down into the water.

What would've happened if I had turned around? Sunk to my knees beside the tub and let my hand drop below the water? It's too easy to imagine.

A crow screeches somewhere above me, and my eyes open. Nothing about my surroundings has changed in the last thirty seconds, except for the heavy breaths streaming from my body. Standing by myself in the woods probably isn't the best place for my daydream, but fuck it. My eyes close again, and my concentration goes back to that moment, and what Natalie's reaction could've been.

I've seen her moan over a slice of dark chocolate cake with her head tipping back and her eyes fluttering shut. In my imagination, this is how she's reacting in the bathtub. My heart is pounding now, in my imagination and in reality.

"Aidan?"

My whole body tenses. Eyes open, I turn. Disappointment rushes through me, even though I knew it wasn't her voice.

Anna stands ten feet away, gazing at me with a lopsided smile. "I thought maybe you'd run away."

"From my own parents' house?"

She shrugs, a shadow of uncertainty dimming her smile.

I feel bad. None of this is her fault. She's a pretty girl, and she thought she was coming here to meet a single man. And it's true. I am single. But am I available? I never saw the distinction between those two words until now.

"Your mom asked me to come and get you. She says it's time for dessert."

For a moment I think Anna might turn and walk away as soon as she's finished delivering my mom's message. I wouldn't blame her if she did. But, no. She waits for me and joins me on the walk up to my parents' house.

"Natalie seems nice. Does she have a boyfriend?"

My forearm muscles tense at the mention of Natalie. "No." My voice is gruff. I could tell Anna that Natalie is fresh from a divorce, but I'm not sure how open Natalie wants to be with that information.

Anna claps her hands twice. "Oh, good. I have some-body for her."

Have somebody for her? Is that a Generation Z way of saying she wants to set Natalie up on a date? I should ask one of my students. Anna is closer in age to them than she is to me. Maybe they'll know.

"You have to discuss that with her. I'm not sure if she's dating right now." We reach the back door and I hold it open for her.

Anna taps my chest with one finger as she passes me on her way into the house. "That I can do."

After dessert, my mom puts *The Christmas Story* on TV.

"It's tradition," she explains to John, Melinda, and Anna.

Natalie excuses herself from the room. For the next ninety minutes, the only movement I make is to sink lower into the armchair I'm sitting in. When the movie is finished, everyone gets up and stretches. Natalie must've gone to take a nap, because she never returned.

John announces they better be getting back, and everyone starts saying their goodbyes. Natalie reappears and says a polite goodbye to my parents' neighbors.

"Good, you're back, " Anna says, placing a hand on Natalie's shoulder. "Aidan said you're single?"

Natalie flinches, taken aback. She glances at me, then back to Anna. "Yes. Why?"

Instead of answering her, Anna turns to me. "Aidan, give me your phone." She gestures at me with fingers that curl in and back out.

I know what she's doing, and it's far easier to let it happen than fight it. Especially with an audience.

Fishing my phone from my pocket, I hand it to her.

Her fingers fly over the screen, and then she presses a

button. A ringing fills the air, and she reaches a hand into a bag and silences it.

"There," she grins, pleased with herself. "We've exchanged numbers. Call me next week and we can all go out."

"Great," Natalie says in a voice that sounds delighted to everyone but me. I happen to know that is Natalie's fake voice.

The neighbors leave, and my mom turns to Natalie after she shuts the door. "I didn't realize you were ready for dating. That's great. Get right back on the horse."

Natalie gives me a dirty look. "Yes, apparently I'll be getting back on the horse with a child."

"Maybe the guy Anna knows is a successful thirty-year-old man."

Natalie raises her eyebrows.

"But probably not," I add. This makes her smile.

My mom rubs Natalie's back. "Nevertheless, it will be good for you." She looks up at my dad. "You ready? Shawn said he was setting up Catan in your office."

"I'm going to kick your ass again," my dad warns.

"Only if you promise to kiss it too." Mom pivots, heading away toward Dad's office, and my dad follows.

"We can probably arrange that," Dad says, smacking her butt as they go.

I groan, but Natalie giggles.

"Where were you during the movie?"

She purses her lips and shakes her head.

"You can't tell me?"

"Nope."

I squint at her, trying to determine if she'll break. She

stares right back at me, and it's clear she's going to keep the secret.

"Fine." I hold up my open palms, showing her I'm giving up. "Do you want to play Catan with my parents?"

"And Shawn?"

I nod.

"Is he staying here too?"

"Probably."

"I'm surprised he's not dating anybody."

"Why?" I lean against the backside of the front door. "Do you want to date him?"

"No." She rolls her eyes. "I was thinking maybe your new girlfriend could set him up. That seems to be her favorite pastime."

I bark a laugh. "Don't ask her to. She probably would. And she's not my girlfriend."

"Try telling her that." Natalie turns on one foot and walks through the entryway. "Come on." She turns back to me, and now she's walking backward. She motions with a curled pointer finger, switching out between her left and right hands. It almost looks like she's dancing.

"I'm coming, I'm coming," I tell her, grinning at her antics. Flashes of my earlier daydream pop into my head, and as hard as I try to push them away, they just won't budge.

14

NATALIE

"Aidan," I whisper, half of my body peering around the open door to his bedroom. It's 12:46 AM. The perfect time for pie.

Aidan doesn't respond. I walk farther into the room until my knees meet the side of his bed. Reaching out, I gently shake his shoulder. "Aidan," I whisper, louder this time.

"Mmmm..." Aidan moans, rolling over onto his back. His eyes open only a little at first, and when he sees it's me, they open fully.

He glances at the clock on the nightstand and lays his head back down on the pillow. "Natalie? What's going on?"

"It's time for pie." I know I don't need any more explanation than that.

"Pumpkin," Aidan mutters, his lower lip popping out.

"Quit pouting and come with me. I have a surprise." Earlier this evening, when Aidan asked me where I'd been while everyone was watching that movie, I didn't answer him. This is why.

Aidan pushes back the covers and sits up. He's wearing

blue and green flannel pajama pants and a white V-neck. His hair is messy as if somebody had been dragging both their hands through it. As I'm thinking that, Aidan really does drag both his hands through his hair, and I wonder if this is something he always does after he wakes.

I step back to allow space for him to stand. He takes in my outfit and smirks.

"It's a nightshirt," I explain, my fingers running over the ivory lace on the end of the sleeve.

"Matronly."

I blow out an annoyed breath and turn for the door. "I'm staying with my best friend's parents. Lingerie seemed like it would be a bit too much."

"No way," Aidan says in voice still thick with sleep. "There is never a bad time for lingerie."

I can think of one million ways to refute his statement, but he would disagree with every one of them, so instead, I choose to keep my mouth shut.

Quietly we creep down the stairs. We both know we don't need to sneak, but it adds to the excitement of waking up for dessert in the middle of the night.

When we reach the first floor, I grab Aidan's hand and pull him to the kitchen. I flip on the lights, and both of us blink at the harshness.

"Here," Aidan says, leaning over and flipping off the light I turned on. He walks a few feet away and flips a different switch. Soft light spills onto the countertops from underneath the top cabinets.

"Better," he says. "Now, where's that pie?"

Grinning, I execute an excited walk with some fancy footwork and make it to the pantry without tripping over myself. Aidan smiles.

"Your silly side is coming back. It's nice to see."

I pause, my hand on the handle of the pantry door. "I didn't realize it went anywhere."

Aidan stays quiet, but only because he doesn't need to say anything more. Of course my sense of humor left. It slowly seeped out of me, dripping all over the wood floor of the apartment Henry and I shared.

Opening the pantry, I step in and retrieve the pie. I walk out, the pie extended and say, "Ta da!"

Aidan's eyes widen. "Is this what you were doing during the movie?"

I nod. "Maple pumpkin pie and cinnamon graham cracker crust with—" I set the pie on the counter and go to the fridge, returning with a glass bowl. "Maple whipped cream."

Aidan places a hand over his heart and groans.

Grabbing plates from the cabinet, I cut two oversized slices and drop a giant mound of whipped cream on the top of them.

Aidan hands me a plate, grabs his own, and leads the way into the living room. He presses a button near the fireplace and flames automatically roar to life.

We both settle onto the couch, our feet propped up on the long gray tufted ottoman.

"Oh my god," Aidan says after taking his first bite. "Heaven."

"Mmmm," I moan in agreement.

"I'm telling my mom you should make the pie from now on."

"Don't you dare." The pie has always been Aidan's mom's thing. I don't want to step on her toes.

After that, neither of us talk. The only sound in the

room is the crackling flames and our forks scraping our plates.

When he's finished, Aidan gets up.

"Where are you going?" I ask.

Aidan looks down at me. He is backlit by the fire and he looks so handsome. If it weren't for his aversion to relationships, he would've been snapped up a long time ago. I know how lucky I am to have him.

"To hide the pie," Aidan grins mischievously. "Sharing is caring, but not when it comes to that pie. I'll be right back," he says, bending down to scoop up my empty plate and fork. I lean back into the couch cushions and take a deep breath.

With a full belly and the fire crackling in this beautiful house, it's the most content I've felt in a long time. I gaze out of the living room windows into the night. It must be a full moon, or somewhere close to that, because moonlight spills through the trees, illuminating the outside chairs and fire pit. Just beyond that is the guest house where Shawn sleeps. I look toward it and see movement through the French doors of the guest house.

Maybe Shawn wants a midnight snack also.

Chuckling lightly, I start to turn away when I see more movement. A second person.

I guess Shawn is already having a snack. A very specific kind.

The second person steps into a swath of moonlight, and everything inside me seizes.

Shawn's hand reaches, caressing the face of the second person, and he leans in for a kiss.

Aidan's dad leans in too.

"Oh my fuck," I say, turning away from them. Embarrassment slips through the cracks in my shock. I wasn't spying on them... I didn't mean to see...

"What's wrong?" Aidan rounds the couch and sits down beside me.

"Nothing," my voice squeaks as I say it. I can't tell him. How do you tell your best friend that his father is cheating on his mother? With his best friend, of all people? Oh my god oh my god oh my god. My fingers are shaking.

I peek at Aidan, but he's not looking at me. He is gazing out of the windows, seeing what I saw.

His jaw is set in a hard line. There is no hint of surprise in his eyes.

"You know?" I whisper.

He rips his gaze away from the guest house. Staring into the fire, there is a hardly perceptible nod of his head.

"How long?"

Aidan doesn't answer, and his jaw remains tense.

My insides start to feel hot, and it's not from the fire. How dare Diego do this to his mom? How dare Shawn? How can a love story as amazing as theirs end up this way?

"Don't you want to kill him? To kill them both? I do." I sit back on the couch, my arms crossed in front of me, and stare at the flames licking against the walls of the fireplace.

The fire doesn't care about this middle of the night revelation, and it doesn't appear as though Aidan does either. Aside from his tension, he doesn't seem that upset.

As a woman, shouldn't I do something? Female solidarity, and all that? Don't I owe it to Aidan's mom to tell her what's happening under her nose? Unless... Maybe she wouldn't want to know.

"Come on." Aidan surprises me by standing up suddenly. He reaches down for my hand and pulls me up with him. Keeping a tight grip on my hand, we walk together across the living room to turn off the fire, both of us avoiding looking out the windows. When the fire is out, and the only light is from the moon shining in through the windows, Aidan looks down at me.

"Can I stay with you tonight?"

I've never seen such vulnerability on his face. "Yes," I hear myself say, even though I haven't taken more than a moment to consider the possible repercussions of what he's asking. He turns, leading me back through the dark house. When we are in my room, he closes the door behind us. This is another line we are crossing, and the air around us is thick with our awareness.

We climb into the bed. The sheets are cold, sending a shiver down my body.

Aidan reaches, pulling me into him. Pushing my hair back from my face, he gathers it into a loose coil and releases it onto the pillow behind me.

We are quiet, our eyes closed. We are breathing the same air, closer to one another than we've ever been before.

Aidan's breathing gets heavier, and before he drifts off, I ask the question that's been running through my mind like NYSE ticker tape. "Why haven't you told her?"

Seconds pass, and I open my eyes. Aidan is staring at me. He opens his mouth, and his whispered answer floats over me.

"She already knows."

I KNEW THE MOMENT AIDAN LEFT MY BED. BEFORE I REACHED over and found his space empty, I sensed he was gone. Perhaps he wanted to save us the awkwardness of waking up next to one another. Much like my question on the night of my drunken bath, we cannot go back. You cannot stop knowing something.

Diego. And Shawn.

The thought flies into my head. Diana knows.

Why? Why does she stay? I don't understand. My heart is a little bit broken. These two people... The greatest love story... The whole world fell in love with their love. A book... A movie... On the outside, they look so perfect.

So similar to my own parents. A pastor who abuses his wife. The main character in an epic love story is gay and cheating on his wife.

I'm not sure what's real anymore.

And Aidan. Poor Aidan. How long has he been keeping this secret? It's no wonder he doesn't believe in the kind of love I read about.

How can I face Diego and Diana this morning? And Shawn? Knowing their secret without them telling me about it first makes me uncomfortable.

To delay my appearance, I take a long, hot shower. I dry my hair until I'm certain every strand is completely dry. I apply makeup, more than usual, and I know that to Aidan this will be a dead giveaway.

There's a knock at my door just as I'm pulling my sweater over my head. Assuming it will be Aidan, I throw it open.

Diana stands there. She smiles consolingly. "Good morning, Natalie. Can I come in?"

Nodding, I step back from the open door. Diana walks in and gestures at the bed. I sit down, and she comes to sit beside me, turning so one foot is on the bed and her other foot is propped on the sideboard. I do the same, turning to face her. Diana's hair is tied in a bun at the nape of her neck, and the ivory blouse she is wearing matches her skin tone.

True to Diana's personality, she doesn't mince words. "Aidan told me what you saw last night."

I nod and swallow, unable to speak.

"He told me you were pretty angry on my behalf." Diana's lips curl into a smile. "I appreciate that."

"He said you already know."

Diana's gaze is soft, her eyes gentle, as though she is handling something delicate. "I have always known."

I gasp, and immediately put my hand over my mouth, then rip it away.

"You don't have to hide your shock, Natalie. It's okay to feel that way." Diana places one hand behind her. Supported by the bed, she leans back and starts talking. "I was twenty-two when I met Diego. He was here on a visa and I had just graduated college. At first, I didn't know he was gay. I was naïve, and he was very, very good at hiding it. By the time I found out, it was too late." She shrugs. "I was already in love with him. And he was in love with someone else." Diana's gaze is glassy, some place far away from this bedroom. "He loved Shawn, but his time in the U.S. was running out. His happiness meant everything to me, so I married him."

Diana looks back at me and winks, patting my knee. "Don't feel bad for me. I got a book and a baby out of it."

The book. I can picture the book on my mother's shelf, with the original cover.

"I didn't set out to lie to people. I'm not even really sure if I did lie. Somebody asked me if it was a book about me and my husband. I said yes. To be honest, I didn't foresee it becoming such a big deal."

"Oh please," I mumble. "You're telling me you didn't know you were sitting on a gold mine of words?"

Diana shakes her head. "I honestly didn't. My heart was broken, and I just needed a place to put my emotions. I wrote a story about my best friend and me, and our road to love. I changed some of the details and never told a soul."

"I won't tell anybody," I assure her. "I don't know if I even believe it yet myself." My head is still trying to wrap around everything. "Can I ask you a question?"

Diana nods, waiting.

"Are you happy?"

She sighs deeply, gazing out the window that overlooks the driveway. "I am now, but I wasn't always. This choice has not been an easy one. There were times when I wanted to give up."

"Why didn't you?"

She looks back to me. "The reasons why I did it in the first place still held true."

"That's very...altruistic of you."

She laughs. "I'm not a nun. There is someone else for me, too. He lives upstate, on a small ranch. Not a working ranch, just two horses and a whole lot of green grass."

I blink hard, trying not to show my surprise. At this point, I'm amazed anything could even surprise me.

"Aidan also told me you brought your manuscript with you. May I see it?"

I stare at her, stupefied. I brought the manuscript hoping something like this would happen, but I never actually thought that it would. *I'm going to kill Aidan. Or hug him. I can't decide.*

I stammer my answer, getting up to retrieve my

overnight bag from where I'd stashed it under the bed after I emptied it. The only thing I left inside was my manuscript.

Terror and excitement take turns for primary emotion as I hand over the spiral-bound stack.

"What's it about?" Instead of looking at the manuscript, Diana fixes her stare on me.

"What's it about?" I echo her question, my voice high-pitched. I wrote all seventy thousand words, but to distill the entire book into a few measly sentences feels impossible.

"I hate that question too, but you're going to have to learn how to answer it." She looks at me expectantly.

"Okay. Um... well." The fingers on my right hand trace a pattern on my jeans. I take a deep breath and try to focus. "It's a love story told in reverse. It starts with a couple meeting to sign their divorce papers. They have with them a box of letters and predictions written to each other over the years. They promised themselves if there were ever a problem with their marriage they would read each other's words before making an irrevocable decision. The story explores the fragility of marriage and how even the tightest connection can be weakened, and the reader will see what a lifetime together can truly amount to."

Diana's eyes are rapt, her attention still on me. "What happens in the end? Do they end up getting a divorce?"

A satisfied smile creeps on to my face. "You'll have to read the book."

Diana pretends to fan herself with my manuscript. "You got my attention. Do you mind if I read it?" She lifts the manuscript a few inches into the air.

"Yes," I shout, my hands flying above my head in excitement.

Diana laughs and stands. "I assume you're hungry?

Aidan was starting to make parfaits before I came up here. He said you like the fancy kind. I'm not sure what that means."

"He's probably re-creating something from a restaurant we go to."

Diana smiles. "He loves you."

The smile falls from my face. "What?" Memories of how I spent half the night flood my mind.

"What? You know he loves you. You are the only person he spends time around other than those roommates of his."

And Allison. But that will be over soon, if it's not already.

"Right," I say, trying to recover. "You caught me off guard, that's all. Of course I know he loves me."

Getting up from the bed, I adjust my sweater and follow Diana out of my room. She pauses at the top of the stairs and places a hand on my wrist. In a low voice, she says, "Everyone knows you know. You might see them act differently now. Though honestly, I'm not sure. This is uncharted territory for us."

She starts down the stairs, and I follow, mentally preparing myself for whatever changes I'm about to walk into.

15

NATALIE

"I HAVE A SURPRISE FOR YOU," AIDAN ANNOUNCES. SETTING his mug of steaming hot coffee on the table, he takes a seat across from me and looks at me with a serious gaze.

I look at Aidan's dad and Shawn for a clue as to what Aidan is talking about, but they only shrug. It's been twenty-four hours since everything with them was out in the open, and not a lot has changed. I had prepared myself for an about-face of behavior. Turns out, I didn't need to.

"What?" My trepidation can clearly be heard. Years of knowing Aidan has taught me to be wary when he announces surprises.

Aidan plucks an apple slice from the cutting board in the middle of the table and pops it in his mouth. He chews, swallows, then says, "We are going on a bike ride."

I point beyond the walls of this nice, warm house. "Out there? No way. It's freezing."

"That's what jackets are for. And hats. And gloves. And scarves."

"How do you know I brought all those things?" I raise my eyebrows at him.

"Even if you didn't, my mom has all that too." Aidan sits back, his eyes on me. I get the feeling he's waiting for me to continue to challenge him.

Pointing outside again, I say, "I'm not riding on that road. There are people in Porsches who drive way too fast."

Aidan laughs and shakes his head. "I found a bike trail on Google Maps. Are you done arguing yet?"

Shawn gets up from the table. "I don't know if she'll ever be done arguing." He winks at me and walks from the room, Aidan's dad following him out.

Grabbing the remaining apple from the cutting board, I push back from the table and rise. "Let me grab my jacket. And all my other winter gear." I make a face as I say it.

"Meet me out front in five minutes. I'll fill water bottles for us."

I head upstairs, unsure why Aidan wants to exercise in the cold.

I make it out front ten minutes later, bundled up in all my cold-weather clothes.

"You're late," Aidan says, opening up the passenger door of his dad's Range Rover.

"Did you know people dressed as marshmallows are more likely to fall down the stairs?" Carefully I climb inside the car and place my hands on my knees, turning to look at Aidan. He stands with one hand propped on the door frame, his mouth open.

"You fell down the stairs?"

"No. I caught myself."

Relief washes over his face. Wagging his finger at me, he

says, "No falling off the bike." The door shuts before I can answer him.

"I can't promise that," I say to the empty car. I don't think I've ridden a bike since high school.

Aidan gets in and starts the car. He starts driving, and I turn around to look for the bikes.

"They're attached to the back. There's a bike mount."

"I didn't realize your dad is a biker." I pause, catching my bottom lip between my teeth as I try and find the right word. "Cyclist? Is it called a cyclist? Bikers wear leather chaps. I think."

Aidan makes a right turn out of the driveway and onto the main road. "He and Shawn ride bikes. And, yes, they would be called cyclists."

"Got it," I nod, tucking my hands between my knees.

"My mom said she started your manuscript last night."

My heart does a flip-flop. I haven't seen Diana since she said goodnight to us last night before heading up to bed. She wasn't at breakfast this morning.

"How does that make you feel?" Aidan glances at me, then back to the road.

"Terrified."

"Why? Your work is great."

"According to one person."

"My opinion doesn't count?" Aidan grabs his chest with his right hand. "I'm hurt."

"You know what I mean." I picture Diana in her favorite armchair, curled up and flipping the pages of my manuscript. "What if she hates it?" The thought makes me want to wretch right here in this fancy SUV.

"She might."

"Aidan!"

He rolls his eyes. "She won't. But you have to have thick skin. Some people will love it. Some people will hate it. It's the nature of the beast."

"I know, but..." My voice trails off. That manuscript, it's my baby. My pride and joy. It's where I've poured my heartache and my euphoria. "Can I include some kind of disclaimer in place of a dedication?" I'm only half kidding.

Aidan chuckles. "Let's pretend you can. What would it say?"

"Please be kind. A real human with feelings wrote this."

Aidan makes a left turn with one hand. The other runs over the stubble on his chin. "I was thinking of something more direct."

"Like?"

"*Don't be an asshole.*"

"Asshole behavior is subjective."

"True. I guess we're going with your disclaimer then."

Aidan pulls into a small parking lot where three other cars are parked.

"You ready for this?" He offers me a fist across the center console.

"No," I respond, bumping his fist with my own anyway.

We get out and Aidan unhooks the bikes from the rack.

"Get on." He pushes one bike toward me. "I need to make sure the seat isn't too high before you start to ride it."

I do as he says, then climb off so he can make adjustments. When he's finished, he places the tools in the back of the car and pushes a button on the trunk. Aidan ducks out of the way and it closes on its own.

"Here." He hands me a helmet. I take it, making a face.

"Safety first, Natalie." Aidan makes a show of placing his own helmet on his head and buckling it below his chin.

I do the same, mumbling, "Don't use your teacher voice on me." I know wearing a helmet is the right thing to do, but an immature, superficial part of me thinks I look goofy.

Swinging a leg over his own bike, he climbs on and places one foot on the ground beside him. He gazes at me expectantly, so I follow suit, using my left foot to push up the kickstand. I wobble at first, but a moment later my muscle memory takes over.

Aidan has already taken off, but I'm slow to catch up. After a minute of pedaling I feel more confident, and quickly I'm up to speed with Aidan. Whoever maintains this path does a good job. It's mostly free of rocks and leaves. The cold air whips my face.

For the most part, Aidan leads the way. I don't mind. He seems to know where he's going, and I have no idea.

After a while, Aidan pulls off to the side. He reaches between his legs and pulls out a bottle of water from his bottle mount. He nods to my bike, and I follow his eyes. Below me, snuggly fitted in a holder, is a bottle of water.

"Thank you for putting that there," I tell him, grabbing for the water and taking a big drink. I'm more than a little exerted. Walking around New York City isn't the cardiovascular event I thought it was. Then again, it doesn't help that I am catching cabs and Ubers more than I probably should.

"Want to go a little more?" Aidan asks. The wind picks up and sends my hair swirling around my face.

"Sure," I say, attempting to spit hair out of my mouth.

Aidan leans over and pushes my hair back from my face. His hand lingers just a fraction of a beat too long.

"Are you mad at me?"

His question confuses me. "Why would I be mad at you?"

"Because I didn't tell you about my parents."

"Not at all. It wasn't your secret to tell."

He gazes at me but says nothing. Suddenly he jumps on his bike and takes off.

It takes me a moment to get my bearings, and in that time Aidan is already far ahead of me. I have to race to catch up, and Aidan keeps turning around to check on me.

"You okay back there, Maxwell?" Aidan yells out.

Hearing my maiden name takes me by surprise, and I falter. Regaining my balance, but not my composure, I keep pedaling.

We ride on for another ten minutes, and Aidan pulls off to the side of the path again. This time he gets off the bike. I do too, removing my helmet and shaking out my hair.

"It's fun, right?" Aidan smiles as he speaks and unbuckles his helmet. He pulls it off, and his hair sticks up everywhere.

I walk over, reaching out and running my hand through it. My fingers close over a small section and I lift it up. "I don't think I've ever seen your hair so long. You should get a haircut before the wedding this afternoon." I let go of Aidan's hair and step away.

"I already called the barber my dad likes and he doesn't have any openings today." Aidan shrugs. "I guess I'll just be scraggly in all of their pictures."

"I could cut your hair," I offer. I've never done it before, but it doesn't look that hard.

Aidan eyes me. He doesn't need to ask if I've ever cut hair. He knows I haven't.

"Okay," he says.

My eyes fly open. I didn't really think he'd agree. "Great," I say, feigning confidence in my ability.

Aidan reaches down and grabs his water bottle, holding it out as if to toast me. I grab my own and tap it against the bottom of his. We finished drinking and get back on our bikes. It's downhill, so it's easier going back than it was coming in. We don't stop again until we reach the car.

Aidan attaches the bikes to the rack, and we leave. After we start to drive, Aidan asks, "Are you ready to go watch Malachi and Karis make the worst decision of their lives?"

"Aidan, seriously? Some people really do get happy endings."

"Yeah, but only if they go to the massage parlors where they have a secret menu."

This time, I don't hold back. I slug him right on his upper arm.

He groans, pretending like it hurt.

I give him a dirty look. "You're foul."

He holds up one hand while the other is on the steering wheel. "Guilty as charged."

Crossing my arms, I turn to look at him as he drives. "Things didn't work out for me and Henry. Things did not work out for my parents. And your parents... Well, they have a very unique relationship. But that doesn't mean all relationships fail."

"All the relationships you just listed looked good on the outside. And look how broken they were on the inside. What hope does anyone have if even the best-looking matches fail?"

"Honestly, Aidan? I don't know. All I know is that it's worth finding out."

Aidan stares at me. His eyes are unfathomable, full of things he can't say, won't say, maybe even things he cannot begin to decipher.

* * *

We are in Diana's bathroom. It's monstrous, a long countertop with two sinks on one side, a large tile shower on the opposite side of the room, and in the center is an over-sized, clawfoot tub. I came in here ahead of Aidan and prepared the space. Between one of the sinks and the tub is a stool, and I've laid a towel out on the edge of the tub. We stopped at the drugstore on the way home from our bike ride and picked up a pair of trimming shears. They lay on top of the towel, gleaming in the overhead light.

Aidan lowers himself onto the stool and stretches out his left leg. The palm of his right hand comes to rest on his right thigh.

"Just a trim," I warn him, gesturing with the second item we purchased at the drugstore: a spray bottle. "Don't ask me for anything complicated."

"Don't stress," he says. He leans forward and shakes his head until all his hair is falling forward and almost covering his eyes. "It's more difficult to see mistakes with hair this long."

"Unless I accidentally take off a chunk." I'm only joking, but I pray that my words don't come true.

Aidan grabs the towel from the counter and drapes it around his shoulders. Pointing the water bottle at his head, I press the button and walk around him in a slow circle, my left hand scraping through his hair to separate it and make sure it's wet. When I'm satisfied, I run a comb through it the way I remember my father's barber did to him. I hated going with him to those appointments, but right now I'm happy he made me go.

Swapping the spray bottle for the scissors, I step in front of Aidan.

The moment I step in between his legs, the air changes. It's heavy, thickened with possibility. My stomach flutters as if there are waves inside my core. Aidan's breathing has accelerated, I can see it in the rise and fall of his chest, more rapid than it was only a few moments ago.

Forcing my arms to work, I lift a section of hair and run the comb through it, then capture it in between the sides of two fingers. My scissors are poised to cut when I feel his hands on the backside of my thighs. My body stiffens, including the hand holding the scissors.

Slowly, so agonizingly slowly, Aidan's hands run up the length of my thighs, only to return to my knees. He does this two more times, and somewhere in between his second and third pass is when I feel myself relax just a tiny bit. I place my scissors onto the countertop.

Tentatively I reach for his hair. Just a few moments ago I was touching him with the imprecise movements of an amateur barber, but now my touch is different. Seeking. Exploratory. Mild shock, the good kind. My fingers run through his soft, overgrown tresses, his hair so silky it slips through my fingers.

Aidan's hands move again, this time to the insides of my thighs, climbing high enough to make me ache. Can he hear my heartbeat? It's thundering in my chest, louder than a stampede of horses could ever be.

His hands pause, and he takes the deepest breath I've ever heard. With his inhale he breathes in the heavy, lusty air that is ripe with possibility, and with his exhale he replaces it with prudence and frustration.

My fingers still as his body sags. He leans his forehead against the bottom of my chest.

His words are muffled, but still I understand him. "You are my girl, Natalie."

With those words, he has ended this. It's his way of reminding me that I am too special, too important for there ever to be anything between us. He will not risk me. He will not risk us.

I step back from him, and his arms fall limply to his sides. I want to run and hide, but I don't.

I stand strong in front of him, my gaze on his. I see not only my best friend, but the man who has stayed by my side while I've loved and lost, made hard rights and easy wrongs. I cannot risk him either. Of all the things I could lose in this world, he can't be one of them.

"I'm going to get ready." My voice is steady, even though the inside of me feels like it's in the middle of an earthquake.

I turn and walk out quickly because I don't want him to see my tears.

16

AIDAN

"You look nice, honey," my mom says, coming in through my open bedroom door.

"Thanks." I turn back to the mirror over my dresser.

"How did your haircut go?" She examines my head.

"Fine," I lie. It most definitely wasn't fine.

"It doesn't look like she took very much off."

"Just a trim," I tell her.

Mom nods. "Are you okay?"

"All good." Grabbing my sports coat off the desk chair, I shrug it on and smile at her. "Promise."

My mom isn't buying it. "You look...weird. And so did Natalie when I saw her downstairs a few minutes ago."

"Thanks, Mom," I say sarcastically.

Mom blows out a short breath. "I didn't really mean you look weird. More just, your aura or your energy, or something like that. You get what I'm trying to say."

I slip my feet in my shoes and bend down to tie them.

"Those are cute," my mom says, probably trying to make up for her weird comment.

"Thanks." I finish tying the laces on my leather tennis shoes and stand up.

My mom takes the hint and backs out of the room. On my way out I grab my keys and my wallet from where they lie on the dresser. My phone is already in my pocket. I stowed it there just before my mom walked into my room, and right after Allison called and I sent it to voicemail. She's probably calling because she's drunk and alone.

"Natalie's in the kitchen," my mom says, walking downstairs with me.

I find Natalie standing near one of the kitchen windows, a glass of white wine in her hand. She holds it out as I approach.

"Nerves," she laughs softly.

"Are you nervous about going to the wedding because of what you've been through recently?" my mom asks her.

Natalie, with her eyes squarely on mine, says, "Mm hmm."

I'd bet three month's salary, which isn't much but is sorely needed by me, that Natalie's nerves are about something else entirely.

"That's perfectly normal," my mom says, stepping in between me and Natalie and wrapping an arm around her shoulders.

Natalie's wearing a long sleeve burgundy dress. It hits at her knees, and with the black heels she's wearing she looks taller. Natalie turns and walks toward the island, and my stomach nearly drops out of me. The back of the dress is missing.

"So pretty," my mom says, running a finger across the top of Natalie's back. I feel ridiculously jealous of that finger. "I love dresses that are subtly sexy."

"Thanks," Natalie murmurs, running one hand over her hip.

I am insanely jealous of that hand too.

Which is incredibly stupid, considering I'm the one who stopped what was happening in the bathroom earlier. I had my reasons, and they were good. Namely, don't fuck up my friendship.

That still holds true, even now as I stand here, turning green on the inside.

Natalie sets her half-empty wine glass on the counter and looks at me. "Ready?"

"Can I get a picture of you two?" My mom laughs and puts a hand over her mouth like she's embarrassed for asking. "When do you two ever get a chance to dress up? Moreover, when do I ever get a chance to see you two dressed up?"

We both agree, and Mom shuffles us over to the fire-place. "It's kind of like prom," Mom says, smiling and holding out her iPhone. She takes a dozen pictures before Natalie tells her that her cheeks are starting to hurt from smiling.

Mom laughs. "Okay fine, I'll stop."

Natalie scoops her purse and coat off the couch. I grab the keys to the Porsche and kiss my mom on the cheek.

"Bye," she yells after us. "Don't drink and drive. Let me know if you need a ride."

Suddenly it hits me that my dad and Shawn aren't around. I don't know where they are, but I feel bad for my mom. She's alone on a Saturday night. The anger that I so often feel when I think of their situation bubbles up. They claim their agreement works for them, but I can't see how.

All three of them are always lying, and all three of them spend a lot of time lonely.

"You seem like you're in deep thought," Natalie says after we've started driving.

Grateful to not be talking about us, I tell her exactly what I was thinking. "I wish they would give up the charade. My whole life I've been lying to people, and I fucking hate it. I can't imagine how they feel."

"It must suck almost as much as people who lie to themselves."

I cast her a quick glance. "Are you referring to me?"

"Yes."

"What am I lying to myself about?"

"Everything."

"Everything?"

"You've convinced yourself that your parents' unusual arrangement is somehow representative of all relationships."

I shake my head. "Not true. I am well aware that a vast majority of the population does not have an arrangement like my parents."

Natalie shakes her head too. "I'm not talking about the details. I mean overall. You've convinced yourself that if love looks like what your parents have, and what my parents had, then you don't want it."

"Why would anybody?"

"Because that's not what love is," Natalie yells, lifting her hands in the air and shaking them.

"Isn't it? What my mother's doing for my father isn't love?"

Natalie blows out a heated breath. "No. Well, yes. It is.

Just not the kind I'm talking about. I'm talking about romantic love."

I'm going to regret asking my next question, but I ask it anyway. "What's your idea of romantic love? And don't give me this hearts and flowers bullshit from your romance novels. I want the real answer. What makes love worth dying over?"

Natalie doesn't respond. I glance at her and find her looking out her window. "Nat?"

She keeps her gaze outside. In two minutes we will be at the hotel where the wedding is taking place, so I don't push her further.

Never has quiet sounded so loud.

I don't know what's going through her head, but I know what's going through mine, and it doesn't feel very good.

Pulling into the hotel parking lot and up to the valet feels like a joyous event. A teenage boy wearing khaki slacks and a black jacket runs over. He opens Natalie's door first, then circles around for mine.

Natalie waits on the curb while I give him my last name and he gives me a ticket.

We're a few steps into the hotel when Natalie puts a hand on my arm and stops me.

"I don't know. My answer to your question is, I don't know." Emotion reverberates through Natalie's voice. "And I don't know with who, but I am going to find out."

Pain. I feel it everywhere. Natalie's words have reached inside me, their meaning searing my heart.

She is going to find out. It just won't be with you.

For the first time in my life, I understand my mom's choice. She loved my father so deeply that she would take him any way she could have him. Of course I would do the same for Natalie.

I've always known a heart was beating inside my body. It's just one of those things you have to trust, because all the signs are there. But in this moment, I feel my heart in a way I never have before. It hurts.

Is this heartbreak? And if it is, don't you have to first love somebody before you can ever feel this way?

I've passed up three separate offers from three beautiful women. Two of them asked me to dance. The third asked if I'd like to fuck a bridesmaid. She was definitely drunk, and definitely willing, and I definitely am not interested.

Natalie is having enough fun for the both of us. She has danced with the bride, the groom, and for the last three songs, she has danced only with the groom's brother. She is not trying to make me jealous. That's not how Natalie operates. She is only trying to forget.

Forget what happened in the bathroom.

Forget my words in the car.

Forget *me*.

It's not easy for me to see her in someone else's arms. Two nights ago, she slept in my arms. I woke up first the next morning, a little stunned to find myself in Natalie's bed. It took only a second for everything from the middle of the night to come back to me. I stared at her sleeping face, wondering why neither of us were trying harder to stay within our carefully erected boundaries. Between that night and today's close call in my mom's bathroom, we are coloring outside of the lines.

The song ends, and a slower one starts. Natalie steps away from the groom's brother, but he catches her hand and pulls her back in. Natalie laughs and wraps her other arm around his shoulders. I look away, out to the dark night beyond the large banquet room windows. My jaw is so tense that my teeth grind together.

Given the way I feel, I'd say the lines in mine and Natalie's relationship have been erased. We are operating in no man's land, a landscape of pure white, unmarred by mistakes and bad choices. Whatever happens from here will leave the first mark.

I don't know what makes me look back to the dance floor, but I'm certain I've made better choices. The guy dips Natalie back, and when he brings her back up again, he kisses her cheek.

I'm out of here.

I push back from the table and stand, but Natalie's eyes find mine. They are wide and worried, heavy with something. Lifting my drink in a salute to her, I drain what little is left of my Crown and Coke. Her head lifts up from that asshole's chest, and even as I turn and walk away, I feel her gaze on my back.

Exiting the reception hall, I keep going down the long hallway and out the double doors at the end. Cold air blasts my face, but right now I welcome the temperature. Two hundred yards away is a small greenhouse. I noticed it on the map in the lobby when we first arrived. This is where I'm headed now. I'll wait for Natalie in the warmth and humidity, and pretend I'm on a beach somewhere tropical. Anywhere but here right now.

Stepping into the greenhouse is like stepping away from cold New York. Miniature trees sit in pots on the ground, plants with long, hanging vines brush my face. The space is maybe twenty feet long, and only ten feet across. At the back is a wooden table, tall like a pub table but longer. Beneath it lay bags of gardening soil.

Tucking my hands in my pockets, I take a deep breath and try not to think of the person who has confused my heart so deeply that even I cannot recognize it.

"What the hell, Aidan?"

I whip around and see Natalie standing there. Both of her shoes are held in one hand. Her eyes are glassy, and all of her hair is tucked over one shoulder. She is barefoot and beautiful. Achingly beautiful. I've always known that Natalie is gorgeous, but it's never done this weird thing to my insides. It's never caused my chest to constrict, my heart straining inside it.

"Where's your new boyfriend?" It's a childish question. I feel raw and exposed.

Her shoulders lift, then drop. "Is that what you want to talk about right now?"

I shake my head at the same time I pinch the skin between my eyes.

"Is there something else you want to talk about?" Natalie steps closer.

I hold out a hand. "Don't come any closer."

"Why?" She slinks forward anyhow.

"This isn't safe." I take a step back, but I know what's behind me, and I can only go so far. So instead of letting myself get pushed up against a table, I stand my ground. "We are going to cross a line, Natalie. Up until now, we have been good at staying within them."

She stops a foot away from me. "You mean up until two nights ago we have been good at staying within them." She tips her head up and to the side as if she's thinking. "Technically, the first line was crossed that night I asked the question from my bathtub. Or maybe that was only toeing the line." She sticks one pointed foot out between us and draws an arc over the concrete with her toes. Looking up at me, she smiles softly. "Do you really believe they're still lines, Aidan?"

"No," I admit. But without lines, what will Natalie and I become?

"You touched me today. You touched my thighs. You ran your hands up and down my thighs and—"

"I'm sorry. I shouldn't have done that. I don't know what I was thinking."

Just like in the car on our drive here, Natalie explodes again. "I don't know what you're thinking either, because you won't tell me. We might be best friends, but I'm not a mind reader. If you want me to know what you're thinking, you need to tell me." Natalie's hands are flying around, gesturing with her frustration.

"Fine," I growl. Now I'm gesturing too. "What's going through my head is fucking terrifying. And I don't know if it's good, or bad, or somewhere in the middle."

Natalie lifts her chin and crosses her arms. "Try me."

"You were married. It was easy to categorize you. *My married best friend*. That's all. But then, your marriage failed. Suddenly you were single, and feelings I've never given attention to were resurfacing, and screaming to be heard. And then that night, when you asked that question? It disabled everything else inside me." My hands make a circular motion over my chest. "Everything ground to a halt.

I didn't understand what I was feeling. I still don't. I only know that it's happening right" —I make a fist and lightly pound the center of my chest— "here."

While I was talking, Natalie's cupped hands rose to cover her mouth. Now, they slowly slide down and she speaks. "That," she says, her voice sliding out just a touch above a whisper, "is romantic love."

"I know," I choke out.

Natalie steps into me, closing all distance between us. She stares up at me, her lips parted, but I can't do what I'm supposed to do because I'm trembling. I'm fucking trembling.

Natalie. This is Natalie. What the fuck am I doing?

But this isn't just Natalie. She isn't the girl I met in high school. She isn't the girl who dated the football star in college, she isn't the girl who became a wife. She isn't the wife who got divorced. She is Natalie. She is my best friend. She's a grown-up. She's a woman. And I'm in love with her.

I place my quaking hands on either side of Natalie's face, and I press my lips to hers. She wraps her arms around me, her hands on the back of my head, and she kisses me back. When my lips part, she is ready. Our tongues touch and I feel the reverberation of her groan. She is not embarrassed or shy or frightened of what's happening.

Spinning us around, I walk her backward until we hit the table. She squeals, and I lift her so she's seated on top. Like she did to me earlier during my failed haircut, I step in between her legs, causing her dress to ride up her thighs. Her hands run over my shoulders and down my sides, then across my stomach. My hands are in her hair, skimming over her collarbone, running the length of her arms.

"Room," Natalie murmurs against my lips.

"Are you sure?" *Please don't let that question change your mind.*

"Room," she repeats.

I don't need to be told a third time. Stepping back, I offer Natalie a hand. She takes it and hops down. I lead her quickly out the door, swiping her shoes from the ground on our way out. The greenhouse door clangs shut behind us.

Our pace is hurried, our feet tripping over the stone pathway. I pause at the entrance to the reception hall. The last time I came through here, I was hurrying for a very different reason. I bend down and set Natalie's shoes on the ground before her. She steadies herself with her hands on my shoulders and slips her feet into her shoes.

Squeezing her hand, I lead her into the hallway, casting a quick glance in the direction of the reception as we pass it. Maybe Malachi and Karis aren't so crazy after all.

"Natalie?"

I stop abruptly at the sound of Natalie's name coming from another man's mouth.

The jilted groomsman stands two steps out of the restroom, a paper towel still balled up in one hand. He looks at Natalie's hand in mine and his eyebrows draw together.

"What's going on?" His eyes are on me now.

"Beckett, this is my best friend." Natalie turns to me. "Aidan, this is Malachi's brother Beckett."

Beckett relaxes when he hears Natalie call me best friend.

"Beckett, thank you for the dances," Natalie continues. "They were fun. Aidan and I are going to take off now. Have a nice night." Without waiting for a response, Natalie pivots on her heel and starts walking away.

I start after her without a backward glance at Beckett.

We round a corner, and Natalie presses her back against a wall and laughs.

"That was awkward. I feel bad."

"Don't. He won't be lonely long." I can think of three girls in particular who wouldn't mind keeping him company.

Natalie still has her back pressed to the wall. She looks like a gorgeous piece of art, one of those real life contemporary pieces that you come upon in a park somewhere.

"Have you changed your mind?" I ask.

Her tongue darts out and swipes against her lower lip, leaving it glistening. "No. Have you?"

Stepping back, I offer her a hand. She takes it and peels herself away from the wall and into my side.

When we get to the front desk, I pull out my credit card and push it across the counter to the front desk attendant.

"One room, please."

The attendant glances at Natalie, then back to me. "One king or two full?" He keeps his expression flat, but I see the confidence in his eyes. He already knows the answer.

"King," I say.

"Yes, sir." The man types quickly, looking down at his computer screen.

He recites the total and I nod, but Natalie balks. "Aidan, that's too expensive," she murmurs, her lips lightly pressing against my shoulder.

"Shhh. It's fine."

The cost of the room is nearly the same as my portion of a month's rent. I have savings, which admittedly doesn't have much in it. This night, however, is worthy of using my trust fund.

The transaction wraps up, and the guy slides the key

card across to me. I slip it in my pocket and nod at him. I'm sure our lack of luggage has not escaped his attention. I'm also certain this isn't the first time he has seen that. Or the fiftieth.

We move to the elevator. There is an energy between us, a sizzling electrical current. It travels over me, pressing into Natalie through our intertwined fingers.

We share the elevator with four other people: one couple, and two men dressed in business attire. We stand at the back, Natalie pressing her body into my side. My free hand runs the length of her back, left bare by her dress.

We are the first to reach our floor. The people part for us to get off, and I wonder if they notice our lack of luggage also. Then again, we could already be settled into our rooms and coming from dinner. Nobody knows us or what this means. Nobody knows the pool we have already dipped our toes into or the fact that we are about to dive in headfirst.

We get to our room and I slip in the key card. It flashes red twice, then green. Natalie giggles nervously.

I push open the door and Natalie steps through. She removes her shoes and drops her purse on a chair. The door slips into place behind me, the lock sliding across with a soft thud.

I'm not sure how to close the few feet that separate us. It is not a great distance, and yet it is. What I'm really crossing are lines, not mere inches. The weight of it keeps me rooted in place.

But not Natalie. My brave, beautiful Natalie. If she fears this, she doesn't show it. She comes to me. She wraps her arms around my neck. She kisses me, her lips coaxing me from my apprehensive state.

Her hands run over my cheeks, scrape along my jaw,

skim over my arms. My own hands are on the small of her back, running up her sides and into her hair. I thought I knew Natalie better than anyone else, and now I see how much more there is to learn.

Natalie tugs lightly on the front of my shirt. Without breaking our kiss, I reach down and grip the backs of her thighs. Her small, surprised gasp steals the air from my mouth. She wraps her legs around my waist, and I carry her to the bed. Gently, I lay her down on the ivory comforter. Her hair spills out around her head, her cheeks rosy.

"You are so beautiful, Nat," I tell her, and she smiles and reaches for me.

I slip her dress down over her shoulders and kiss her skin. I keep going this way, a few inches of dress lowered, followed by my mouth on her exposed skin. Her hands clench in my hair, and in a few minutes time they are gripping the sheets.

I press a kiss to her before sitting up and removing my clothes. When I look down, she's smiling.

"What?" I ask.

"That wasn't weird. It was amazing. But, it's you."

I lie on top of her, supporting my weight on one forearm, and kiss her again. "And you," I tell her between kisses. "Me and you."

I don't get a condom, and she doesn't ask me to. I can't bear to experience Natalie with a barrier. She is my best friend, and I've known her in every way except this one.

I kiss her slowly as I push into her. Her whole body tenses and she moans. I smile against her. I can't help it. It's her dark chocolate cake moan, only better. My movement becomes a rhythm, and Natalie's legs lock around my back.

"Aidan," she groans my name, and I feel like a superhero, like I can do anything in the world as long as this woman is mine.

I keep going, our gazes locked, and hold her as she falls apart beneath me.

Until dawn the next morning, I learn about Natalie.

She likes to be kissed on the back of her neck and the inside of her thighs.

I found her birthmark.

I know that nothing will go back to the way it was before. And I don't want it to.

17

NATALIE

"Where were you two? I was worried. Just because you're grown doesn't mean parents stop worrying. I told you to call me if you needed a ride." Diana stands in the doorway, one arm propped on the jamb and the other firmly on her hip. Her concerned expression is slowly melting away, irritation taking its place.

"Sorry, Mom," Aidan says, walking up the steps and coming to a stop on the welcome mat. He offers no explanation, and I wonder what she will make of that. She peers around Aidan to where I'm standing at the foot of the stairs. My shoulders tuck in as she scrutinizes me, and I ignore the desire to run a hand over my face, as though Aidan's kisses have left imprints.

But they have left a mark. Invisible, but just as permanent.

Diana steps away from the door. I hurry up the stairs and follow Aidan into the house. I long to reach out and touch him, but I can't. When we woke up this morning, we decided we're not ready to tell anybody about us. We want to be alone in our newfound place, cocooned only by our own emotions. The thoughts and opinions of others can come later.

We both head for the kitchen. In an effort to get back to Aidan's house this morning, we skipped breakfast. After last night's physical exertions, it's safe to say we are both more than a little hungry.

Aidan goes right to the fridge, and I go to the pantry. I grab the first thing I see: tortilla chips. Aidan pulls away from the fridge with eggs, sausage, bread, and a canister of cinnamon rolls.

He sees what I'm holding and opens his mouth. I feed him a chip as he unloads everything onto the counter.

"Good idea," he says, leaning down and giving me a quick kiss.

"Aidan," I whisper-hiss, stepping back and looking around. We are lucky this time. Nobody is around to catch us.

He makes a face. "I don't know how long I can keep us a secret."

"Then don't. We could just tell them now." If it means I can touch Aidan when I want to, then maybe it's worth it.

Aidan shakes his head. "Let's stick to the plan." He tucks his chin and leans toward me. In a low voice, he says, "You should expect me to sneak into your room after we eat. I plan to take that dress off you twice."

"Maybe breakfast can wait," I murmur, but then my stomach growls and ruins the moment.

Aidan laughs. "Apparently not."

Making the pumpkin maple pie gave me an introduction into how Diana sets up the kitchen, so I'm lightning fast at getting together everything we need to cook breakfast. While we cook, we snack on tortilla chips.

In twenty minutes we are fed and finished with what is admittedly a shitty job of cleaning up behind ourselves.

Trying to act normal as we walk through the house and to my room is harder than not kissing Aidan in the kitchen. My stomach is flip-flopping more now than it was last night, a feat I wouldn't have thought possible.

The gods are on our side. Nobody is around to see us creep through the house, up the stairs, and into my room. Aidan locks the bedroom door and follows me into the bathroom. He closes that door too, then turns on the shower.

"Shower sex?" I ask.

He pulls me into him and kisses my forehead. "I was doing that for noise, but now that you mention it..."

Aidan pushes the dress from my shoulders. He kisses me, and I lose myself almost instantly. His touch, his scent, just knowing it's *him*, it's all so overwhelming. Now that we are doing this, I can't believe we haven't always been.

Eventually, we make it into the shower.

* * *

"You go out first, then I'll follow a couple minutes later," Aidan tells me the plan as he puts his clothes back on. "I'm going to my room to change and then I'll be down."

"Sounds good." I kiss him one more time and pull my zippered bag over my shoulder. My party dress is safely stowed inside, and I've changed into jeans and a sweatshirt.

He stands back away from the door, and I walk through,

pulling it closed behind me. I'm almost to the stairs when Diana speaks.

"Natalie, there you are."

I whip around. Diana is standing in the hallway, almost right in front of my door.

"Hi," I say loudly, hoping like hell Aidan hears me.

Diana walks closer. "I'm glad I caught you. I wanted to talk with you about your manuscript."

Holy crap. With everything that happened last night with Aidan, I nearly forgot about giving Diana my manuscript.

"You hated it, right? I knew it." I'm not kidding. Crippling self-doubt is a hallmark of all writers.

"Quite the opposite. It has a lot of potential. If you don't mind, I'd like to send it to my editor."

My eyes widen, and Diana raises her hands. "I can't make any promises. There's a lot more to book publishing than a good book, unfortunately. But—"

A cell phone rings. From my bedroom. We both look toward my closed door, then at each other.

"I must have left my phone in the room," I say, but I'm a terrible liar. My voice quivers and I cannot make my gaze stay in one place. Diana is apparently great at detecting lies. She looks at the room again, then back at me.

"The ringing cut off after one ring," she says.

"Damn telemarketers," I say lamely. "Must be that auto-answer thing they have."

Her expression goes from shrewd to shining, and I realize she knows. She stares at me for an extra beat, smiling.

"Assholes," she agrees, letting me off the hook. "So, I'll let you know what my editor says. Sound good?" She starts down the stairs and I follow.

"Sounds amazing," I tell her, setting my bag at the foot of the stairs.

Diana gestures to my bag. "I know you have to get back to the city, but I wish you could stay longer."

"Me too." Suddenly I remember the pie Aidan hid. "I have a surprise for you." I walk to the kitchen and pull open the pantry. Moving aside some boxes, I pull the container from its hiding spot.

"Pumpkin maple." I hold it out to her.

"You made pie?"

"When you all were watching that movie on Thanksgiving Day."

"I thought the turkey had gotten you and you were napping." Diana removes the lid and brings it to her nose, inhaling. "Oh my god. I need this right now." She walks to the cutlery drawer and removes two forks. She takes a bite and moans.

"It's better than mine."

"No way."

She takes another bite, pointing down at the pie with her fork. "Did you make this for Aidan?"

I take a bite and nod.

She smiles. "I'm glad he has you, Natalie. He needs you."

I stuff another bite of pie into my mouth so I don't have to say anything.

Aidan walks in and stops short when he sees us. He strides over and we both hand him the pie. He takes my fork and eats the final slice in complete silence. He groans when he's finished and tips his head back.

Diana laughs, but I have to look away. It's the second time today I've seen him do that.

We thank Diana for everything, and she apologizes that Aidan's dad and Shawn are out and unable to say goodbye.

"We'll be back in the city in a few days," she tells Aidan as she hugs him goodbye.

To me, she says, "I'll call you soon."

Aidan loads our bags into the back of the tiny car, and we get in. Diana waves from the porch until we are gone. As soon as we are out of her sight, Aidan presses on the gas. I squeeze my eyes tight and enjoy the ride.

* * *

WE'VE MANAGED TO KEEP OUR RELATIONSHIP SECRET FOR TWO weeks now. We meet in places neither of us would usually go and hope this means our friends wouldn't go there either. Savannah spends the night at Drew's place often, but not often enough. By the time we're in bed together, we're starving for one another.

New York City is alight with holiday cheer. Last Christmas, I was separated from my husband and living alone in our apartment. It's amazing what a difference a year can make.

Last night was one of our lucky nights. Savannah stayed with Drew and plans to be there all day today. Aidan is snoring softly beside me. I stretch out and look up at the ceiling, laughing silently. Last night Aidan commented that he ended up christening my new bed after all, and I didn't correct him.

Aidan sleeps for another hour. I get up, make coffee, order bagels and cream cheese from the place on the corner, and read the news on my iPad. When Aidan comes out of my room, his hair rumpled and it makes me want to take him right back into the bedroom. He got a haircut soon after we came back from the city, but he still has the best bedhead I've ever seen. Apparently, bedhead turns me on.

"Hey you," he says, climbing onto the couch behind me and wrapping his arms around me. I take a bite of my everything bagel and hand it to him. He reaches over my shoulder and takes it.

"Lizzie's?" he asks.

"Duh," I reply, scrolling for the next headline. Lizzie's makes the best bagels. Once I asked them why theirs are better than everyone else's. They told me what sets them apart is that they boil their bagels. Who knew?

Aidan finishes my bagel and gets up. He pours himself a cup of coffee and slathers cream cheese on another bagel. He sits down beside me and offers me half.

"What are we doing today?" He glances at me and brushes crumbs from his lips.

"Whatever we want." I lean forward and kiss away the spot of cream cheese he missed.

"What do you think about starting the process of changing your name back to Maxwell?"

This is something I've thought a lot about. If Henry and I had had kids, the choice would be much more difficult. We didn't, and there is no reason for me to keep Henry's last name. But going back to Maxwell feels like yet another piece of evidence to show we failed. First the separation, then the divorce, and now going back to my maiden name. There are so many ways in life in which we cannot go back, but in names, we are allowed a redo.

"I've already thought about it. It's just a matter of actually doing it. I made sure it was listed in the divorce decree, just to make things easier on me. If I have time this week, I'll stop by the Social Security office."

"You don't have to do anything you don't want to do."

"I know. But I do want to go back to Maxwell. It's just," I shrug, searching for the right words. "It's just so odd that for four years I was known as something else. Professionally, I've only been Shay."

"Do you want your first bestseller to say Shay or Maxwell?"

"Maxwell." I didn't even have to think about my answer.

"There you have it."

I sweep my hands together as if I'm brushing off the problem. "So easy."

Aidan plucks the iPad from my hands and sets it on the table beside his empty plate. Pulling me into him, he rests his chin on the top of my head. "I'm sorry. I didn't mean to put pressure on you."

"You didn't. Going back to my maiden name makes sense. I want to do it. I guess I'm still little shocked that my marriage failed. Not that I miss Henry," I hurry to say. "When I'm eighty-five, and I look back over my life, my first marriage will be part of what I think of. If our lives are like a beautiful tapestry, and mine is still on the loom, then that part of my life has already been woven in. Does that make sense?"

"I understand your words, but I don't relate to them at all. As you obviously know, I've never been married. Which means I've never been divorced. What I do know, is that every single person has a tapestry. And every tapestry looks different. Some tapestries will have four or even five marriages. Some will only have one, or none. Who's to say which one is better? Who's to say that either one of them is bad?"

I pull back so I can look at him. "You're very wise."I run my fingertips over his face, inspecting.

"What are you doing?"

"Looking for wrinkles. Somebody so wise should have more wrinkles."

Without warning Aidan dips me back, and we tumble together on the couch. "I'm forever young," he says, his fingertips brushing over my stomach. I laugh and twist, trying to escape his tickling fingers.

"There's no way I'm letting you go." His teeth nip my collarbone, his hand drifts lower.

This is the kind of Sunday I could get used to.

18

AIDAN

For someone who's never considered himself a romantic guy, I'm not doing too bad of a job.

"Thank you for lunch," Natalie says, leaning into me. She plants a kiss on my cheek before bending over and lacing up her ice skate.

"Of course," I tell her, lacing up my own ice skates. When I'm finished, I straighten up and lean back on the bench, surveying all the happy ice skaters on the rink in front of us. It's picturesque. The rink in Central Park, the barren trees with the buildings towering all around them.

Natalie pops up from the bench. I can already tell her balance is better than mine.

"When was the last time you've done this?"

"Last winter, with the girls from work. They were trying to cheer me up. When was the last time you've been?"

"Not since I was a kid." I push off from the bench, wobble, and grab onto the side of the rink. Natalie giggles.

"You have to promise not to laugh if I fall."

She shakes her head. "I will make no such promises."

I scowl and she laughs again. She holds out a hand. "I promise to stay beside you and hold your hand. If you go down, I'll go down with you."

I place my hand in hers. "Deal."

We step out onto the ice, and after a few minutes, I realize it's not that bad. There're other things I'd rather be doing, but this isn't the worst thing in the world. We stay on the outside of the crowd so that I can grab the wall when I feel unsteady. Natalie seems content to skate slowly beside me. In the center of the crowd are the real ice skaters. They twirl and do small jumps. Though there are no tracks in the ice, everyone seems to skate inside an invisible lane. We go around another time, and this is when it happens. I fall on my ass. And though she told me she would, Natalie does not fall with me.

The cold immediately seeps through my jeans. Natalie covers her mouth with one hand and reaches down to help me with the other. Getting up from the ice might be even harder than staying upright on it. Once I can stand, I make my way to the outer edge of the rink and lean on it. Natalie glides over, dragging her skate sideways to slow her advance.

"Why don't you go around a few times without me? Let me see your skills."

She grins, her cheeks flushed from the cold. "Okay," she says, pushing off and finding her place in the crowd of people passing by. I watch her go around, entranced by her easy grace. It reminds me of being in high school and college and watching her on the dance team. I wonder if she ever misses it. Judging by the look on her face, I think the answer is yes. When she passes me a third time, I point to the benches on the outside of the rink.

Without Natalie, getting there is much more difficult. To

avoid falling, I cling to the wall and slowly make my way to the exit. I don't feel so bad about my less than stellar exit; there are at least seven more males doing the exact same thing. I meet eyes with one of them and we laugh at ourselves. I sit back down and wait for Natalie. My pocket buzzes and I reach for my phone.

Allison?

I open my phone and read her message. **I need to talk to you.**

Closing my phone, I slip it back into my pocket. Allison is a nice person, and I wish her nothing but the best, but we do not need to talk.

Natalie comes off the ice, beaming. The flush on her cheeks is rosier than before.

"That was fun." She comes to sit beside me.

"I'm glad you liked it. I'm ready for some spiced wine. How about you?"

Natalie nods. "Yes, please. I need to thaw out."

This gives me an idea. "How does a hot shower sound?"

Natalie turns to look at me. Her eyes are hooded, hungry. "That sounds delightful." Her face falls. "But we don't have anywhere to go. Savannah will be back soon, and we definitely can't go to your place."

I think for a moment, then pull my phone from my pocket. There is a second message from Allison, but I ignore it. Instead, I text Rob and Aaron and ask them to meet me for a beer. Rob says he's running an errand but can be there in thirty minutes. Aaron says he'll head out and be there in fifteen.

"Change back into your shoes," I instruct, changing out of my ice skates with warp speed. Natalie listens, talking as she goes. "What's going on?"

Slipping my feet in my shoes, I stand and offer Natalie a hand. "I have no idea what my apartment looks like right now. It's probably disgusting. But, it's available."

Natalie jams her feet into her boots and stands up. We dump our ice skates on the return counter and hurry through the park. We dodge people, laughing, and on the way to my apartment we pass the bar I have no intention of going into.

It isn't until later that night, long after Rob and Aaron have given me shit for not showing up, that I remember Allison's second text.

I grab my phone, and the first thing I see is Natalie's face. The picture of her that I used for her dating profile is now my wallpaper. I'm officially one of those guys. My girlfriend is my phone's wallpaper.

We haven't talked about it yet, but we're unofficially boyfriend and girlfriend. She knows it, I know it, we just haven't said it out loud yet.

I navigate to my text and tap on Allison's name. Our conversation appears, and I read her last message. **I know we weren't serious, but please don't ignore me.**

I don't want to deal with this right now. I want to fall asleep reliving my day with Natalie.

So that's what I do. It's so much easier to turn away from a problem than to face it.

THREE DAYS LATER, I FIND THERE IS NO RUNNING FROM MY problem. My problem has come to find me. I see her as soon as I walk out of school. She is across the street leaning on a brick wall. Snow has just started to fall, but it's not the nice kind. It's wet and mushy. Obviously I can't avoid Allison now, so I cross the street and walk up to her, coming to a stop a couple feet away.

Allison stands up straight so she's no longer leaning on the wall. She glances at the school behind me, then her eyes meet mine. Her fingers tap out a rhythm on her arm, and she bites the side of her lower lip.

"Allison?" I say her name, hoping it will prompt her to speak.

"I'm sorry that I came to your work. I could've gone to your apartment, but didn't want to deal with your room-mates. You weren't answering my texts, and I didn't know what else to do."

Even though she's wearing a big coat, Allison shivers. I realize she's not wearing a hat, so I pull mine off my head and offer it to her. She declines with a shake of her head.

"Can we go somewhere to talk?" she asks, craning her head to look down the street. "There, maybe?" She points at a bakery on the corner.

"Sure." If it weren't for this weather, I'd walk her around the corner from the school and ask her to say whatever it is she's come to say.

We walk beside each other in complete silence. Allison was a nice person, and we had a good time together. From the beginning she knew we didn't have a future. So why is she here now? Did she see me out with Natalie? Does she think it means I changed my mind on relationships?

We settle at a table inside the bakery, and I order two coffees. I sip from mine, but Allison doesn't touch hers. She starts to take off her coat, then changes her mind and keeps it on.

"What do you want to talk about, Allison?" If she won't start the conversation, I will.

She stares at me, her eyes growing shiny. "I've been trying to get in touch with you."

Maybe I should have wrapped it up in a more official way. I thought being casual meant I didn't have any ties, but clearly Allison needed more than my short phone call.

"I'm sorry, Allison. I should've answered your call."

"Thank you," she says, accepting my apology. "Did you mean what you said? That we are finished?"

My jaw clenches. This is painful. And a little frustrating. From the beginning, I made it clear to Allison that I was not looking for a relationship.

"Yes." Does she need to be reminded that her last words to me included telling me to fuck off?

Allison nods. "I see."

I pull my jacket off my lap and start to stand. "Well, if that's all, I better get going."

Allison's hand shoots out across the table. "I'm pregnant."

What.

The.

Fuck.

I drop back down in my seat. Everything inside me feels heavy and hollow at the same time. How can this even be? We used condoms. And I was careful. So careful.

Natalie.

Oh my god. How am I going to tell her? My hands drag through my hair, and I have to control the urge to pull tightly. I want to punish myself for this colossal mistake. This cannot be. This just *cannot* be.

Across the table, Allison watches me absorb the news. "I'm eight weeks along," she says, and this one sentence makes everything even more real. I don't say anything, because I don't trust myself just yet. When I open my mouth, I want to say the right thing, only I don't know what the right thing is.

Allison keeps talking. "It was our last time together. I know what you're thinking, and no, I didn't trap you. This was a surprise to me too."

"That's not what I was thinking." There. My silence is finally broken.

"I'm going to keep it." Allison lifts the cup of coffee to her lips, then sets it back down. "No caffeine," she says quietly as if she's reminding herself.

"Okay."

"You can be as involved as you want."

"Okay."

"First doctor's appointment is in two days. Do you want to come to it?"

"Okay."

Allison blows out a hard breath. "Do you have anything else to say besides *okay*?"

Sure I do. But it involves a lot of expletives and screaming, maybe even punching things, and she doesn't need to see or hear any of that. Pinching the bridge of my nose, I squeeze my eyes tight and murmur, "How am I going to tell Natalie?"

"Natalie?" Allison's eyes are wide, her face shocked. "Natalie, as in your best friend? Why do you care so much about her reaction?" Light dawns in Allison's eyes even as she speaks. She crosses her arms and looks out the window, her eyes teary.

"This isn't how I saw this going," Allison says.

"How did you see this going?"

Allison looks back to me. Two tears have managed to escape her eyes and are rolling down her cheeks.

"We got along well, you know? We smiled, and we laughed, even if we really only met for sex. We had chemistry." She laughs once, a vacant sound. "I had this fantasy where you were happy to hear the news. You were shocked, but you got over it. You wanted to start a relationship with me. We went to doctor's appointments, and my stomach grew bigger." She reaches down and rubs a circle over her midsection. "When you first mentioned Natalie, I thought it was weird you had a girl as your best friend. But after a while, I grew comfortable with that because it didn't seem like there was anything there. And then we saw her on the street that night. I should have known when you said you weren't feeling well after we saw her." She shakes her head. "I should've known."

"When is your appointment?" I want to steer her away from the topic of Natalie.

"Wednesday. Four o'clock."

"Are you sure? That I'm the father?"

Allison's eyes fill with outrage. "You have got to be fucking kidding me," she hisses, her eyes flashing and her top lip curling. She stands, and for a moment I wonder if she'll toss her full cup of coffee in my face. I flinch, preparing for it, but she steps away from the table.

"See you Wednesday, Aidan. I'll text you the address. And in the meantime, fuck off." She stalks away, the tinkling bell above the door signaling her exit.

"Fuck," I mutter, finishing the last of my coffee and tossing it into the trash. I toss her coffee in the trash too, then put on my coat and walk out the door. I stop when I get outside, looking up at the gray sky. It continues to drop globs of wet snow, and if I wasn't so close to my work, I'd lift my hand and give the darkened sky the bird.

There is only one place I can go now, even though everything inside of me is telling me to turn around and go in the opposite direction. Pulling out my phone, I send Natalie a text. We were supposed to meet for dinner, but I've asked her to meet me at her apartment instead. Natalie won't be off work until five, and by the time I make it to her apartment, it's only four thirty. I pass her building, go over one block, and settle at the bar of an Irish pub. If there were ever a time when a man deserves a shot of whiskey, it's right now.

19

NATALIE

"WHY DO YOU LOOK SO HAPPY?" SAVANNAH STANDS AT THE entrance to my cubicle, her forearm resting on the top of the short wall. In her other hand, she holds a cup of chamomile tea.

"No reason," I lie, thinking of Aidan's most recent text message. I wonder why he wants to meet me at my apartment before dinner. *Probably a quickie.* I try not to smile under the scrutinizing glare of Savannah. Maybe right now her own phone is lighting up with a text message from Aidan, and he's pulling a fast one on her like he did to his roommates yesterday. Even though we almost got caught, it was worth it. Rob and Aaron came back before I could get out of there, bitching and moaning through Aidan's door about how he stood them up. We waited for the TV to turn on, and while their backs were turned, I crept like a burglar behind them. When my hand was on the doorknob, Rob noticed me. "Best, when did you get here?" he'd asked me. I turned around, glanced at Aidan, and said, "Just now." Then I stayed for another hour.

Savannah sips her tea, her gaze going below my desk.

"I don't have it," I tell her. I know she's looking for my gym bag.

She pouts. "I'm torturing myself alone tonight?"

"Afraid so."

"What are you doing instead?"

"Don't you have work to do?" I ask.

"You're seeing a guy, aren't you? Is he from your dating app?"

I hold up my hands. "Guilty as charged."

"People from those apps can be dangerous. Where are you meeting him? Someone else should always know where you're supposed to be."

"I'm waiting for him to tell me what restaurant we're going to."

She points a finger at me. "And then you'll tell me."

I cross my heart, and she laughs. Savannah returns to her cubicle, and I glance at the time on my phone. Twenty-four more minutes before I get out of here and haul ass back to my apartment. I can't wait to see Aidan.

* * *

WHEN I ARRIVE HOME, I FIND AIDAN SITTING ON THE GROUND outside my apartment door. His knees are pulled into his chest, and his arms rest on his knees. His gaze stays on the ground, even though I know he can hear me approaching.

"Aidan?" I step closer until I know he can see the toes of my shoes.

He looks up. In his eyes I see something I've been half expecting. Fear. I knew this would happen sooner or later. Aidan has been one way his whole life, but that doesn't mean his recent change of heart doesn't have strings, pulling him back into his prior belief. I'm a little jarred, but since I've been expecting this, it's easier to stay calm.

"Come inside." I reach out a hand to help him up. Aidan shoulders most of his own weight as he stands, but feeling the warmth of his hand in mine brings me comfort. Unfortunately, I have to let it go so that I can let us into my apartment. I take my keys from my bag, then reach around him and unlock the door. He follows me in and watches me put down my things and kick off my shoes. I hang my coat on the coat rack and motion for him to do the same. He shakes his head slightly, and this is what makes the calm in me disappear. *He is not planning to stay.*

"Aidan, what's going on?"

He opens his mouth and closes it as if he can't quite form the words. The longer he stands there, rooted in place only a few feet inside the door, the faster my heart beats. Even though I've just come in from the frigid outside, even though I've taken off my coat and I'm down to just my silk blouse and slacks, my underarms begin to feel clammy.

"Just say it," I snap, losing my patience. I can't handle the look on his face. Even knowing that whatever he is going to say will hurt me, I can't bear to see him in pain.

"Allison," he finally croaks, his head shaking in tiny, rapid pulses, as if he is trying to expel whatever it is that's inside there.

My eyes narrow. "What about her?"

"She's pregnant." His voice is empty, yet his message drills right into the center of me.

My hand reaches out, looking for the couch, but I'm too far away. My legs are weak, incapable of holding me up any longer. I collapse, right onto the hardwood floor. Pulling my knees into my chest, I tuck my chin and try to make myself as small as possible.

This cannot be happening.

Maybe if I keep my eyes squeezed tightly shut, this problem will disappear. I hear the rustle of Aidan's jeans, feel the movement of air displacing as he sits down beside me. His arms wrap around me, tugging me onto his lap. Pressing my face to the front of the shirt, I cry into the soft flannel.

"I can't believe it either." Aidan's voice drifts around me.

After a few minutes, I sit back and look at him. He doesn't look so frightened, now that he has told me. I swipe my cheeks, but the tears I've just wiped away are immediately replaced by more.

"How did she tell you?" My words come out garbled because of Aidan's hands on my face. He pulls them away, settling on my upper arms instead.

"She was waiting for me when I walked out of school this afternoon. She texted me a couple times yesterday, but I ignored them."

We were together all day yesterday. He didn't mention the messages, but then again, why would he?

"She wanted to know if we were definitely over. From the very beginning I told her what to expect, but" —Aidan shrugs slightly— "I guess I hurt her feelings anyhow. Then she told me about... about..."

"The baby," I say for him.

He nods slowly.

A thought pops into my head, and I cling to it as though it is a life preserver and I'm being tossed around in the stormy ocean. "Are you sure the baby is yours?"

"I asked her. She was so insulted. There was a cup of

coffee on the table in front of her and I thought she was going to throw it in my face." Aidan looks down to the front of his shirt, like he is double checking to make sure it really didn't happen. He looks back to me, his eyes wary. "Allison and I had a conversation right after we met. She had just gotten out of a bad relationship and wasn't looking for anything. Obviously, that suited me. She asked me not to sleep with other people if I was sleeping with her." A small smile twists one side of his lips. "She said it was icky."

Despite the awfulness of this whole situation, a small bubble of laughter escapes my throat. I don't know Allison at all, but for some reason, I can picture her using the word *icky*.

The momentary break from the heaviness of the situation is gone, and now everything sits right here again, wedged into the space between our chests.

"Do you think... Is there any way that you... Where do we go from here?" Aidan flinches when he's done speaking, as if he knows the answer but had to ask the question anyhow.

"You already know, Aidan."

His eyes drift off to the side and he nods.

I just went through a divorce, but this hurts more. Henry hurt me a little bit every day. Aidan has just ripped my heart from my chest. And he didn't even mean to.

I know what will happen now. He will fall in love with the baby. Maybe he will fall in love with Allison.

Isn't that the way it should go? I don't know Allison, but I cannot deny her a chance at a family. If I kept Aidan as mine, if I didn't allow him the opportunity to participate in this experience fully, I'd never be able to forgive myself.

Aidan's gaze locks on mine, and my eyes fill up with

tears. In all our years of friendship I've never seen Aidan cry, but right now there are tears rolling down his face.

He slips his hands through my hair and pulls my face to his. He kisses me softly, his lips dancing over mine. He pulls back an inch, and I feel the heat of his breath on my skin.

"You'll always be my Best." His words tumble over me, his double meaning shooting straight into my ripped up heart.

I can't respond. If I dare to open my mouth, the only sound that will come from me will be sobs.

We sit on the floor and hold each other as the city comes to life around us. People are off work, meeting friends for happy hour, going to dinner with their partners. They have no idea that up here in this apartment, a decade of friendship is being tested by life. We made it through my marriage. But this? A baby is bigger than us. Bigger than the day I promised to love Henry forever.

In a tapestry, can pulling on a single loose thread unravel the whole thing?

* * *

SYDNEY CALLS AT ELEVEN O'CLOCK THAT NIGHT AFTER I'VE cried myself to sleep.

"What?" I ask, still half asleep.

"Nothing," Sydney chirps. "Just calling to chat."

"Do you know what time it is?"

"It's not late. I just got done studying."

Sydney's words run on top of one another and it's hard for me to understand her. Either that or I really am still sleeping.

"I was sleeping, Sydney."

"Well, wake up."

I don't have the patience for this. "I'm going back to bed. Goodbye."

"C'mon, don't hang up. I haven't talked to you since Thanksgiving. Don't you want to talk about Mom? How was she? Was she drunk? Ha ha, stupid question. Of course she was. You haven't even asked me how my Thanksgiving was. It was lovely, in case you're wondering. Wait, didn't you go to Aidan's parents fancy Pound Ridge House? How was that?"

Sydney finally takes a breath, and my head is reeling from trying to keep up with all her questions.

"Everything was great. Let's talk tomorrow." There's no way I'm telling her about everything right now. Even though she said she just finished studying, I think she might be drunk.

"Natalie," she whines my name.

"Bye, Sydney." I hang up and switch my phone to do not disturb.

I lie there in the dark, trying my best to fall asleep, but it's elusive. I cannot stop my mind from running in circles, or alleviate the pain in the center of my chest. I get up, open my laptop, and pull up a new braiding tutorial. Once I have all my rubber bands and a brush, I hit play and get to work.

"I'M LOVING ALL THESE NEW HAIRSTYLES," SAVANNAH SAYS, lifting a fishtail braid off my shoulder. She examines the complicated plait, then drops it. It lands against my back with a soft thud.

"Thanks. I've been watching some YouTube tutorials." *Some* is an understatement. I've been watching *a lot* of

YouTube tutorials. It has been ten days since the pregnancy bomb was dropped. Aidan and I talked on the phone the day after he told me, trying hard to communicate the way we did before we took our relationship to the next level, but it was forced and painful. After Allison's appointment, I sent him a text message asking how it went. He confirmed that there is indeed a baby, and it looks a bit like a peanut. I haven't talked to him since that day. I cannot bring myself to pretend everything is fine when *fine* is the last thing I am.

In hindsight, I wish we told everybody we were involved. Because nobody knew about our relationship, it's hard to tell anybody about our demise. My sister is the only person I've told. I called her back the day after her late-night phone call, and she confirmed that after she finished studying, she took two shots of tequila to help her relax. We laughed about it until my laughter was replaced with tears. I told Sydney everything, and never before have I wished so badly that we were in the same city. A hug from her might make me feel a little better. And even a little better is better than how I feel right now.

"Do you mind if I poke through your closet?" We've been sitting on the couch for the last hour watching *House Hunters* and waiting for Savannah's boyfriend to go to work. On Friday nights he tends bar at a swanky uptown place, which means we drink for free. "I'm not feeling my wardrobe tonight."

I wave a hand toward my bedroom. "Have at it."

She claps her hands twice and gets up, going to my room. I follow her in and sit on the bed, watching her inspect my clothes. She pulls out the dress I wore to the wedding and holds it up to herself. Turning right and left, she says, "This is a sexy little number. Where did you wear this?"

"Malachi and Karis' wedding." Even though I'm saying their names, I'm not picturing them at all. Instead I see Aidan in the greenhouse with confused emotions tumbling through him, scooping up my shoes and leading me to the hotel, rocking above me in the bed. My eyes tighten and burn at the memories. I turn away and fiddle with something on my nightstand so Savannah won't see how upset I feel.

"Who?" she asks. Hangers scrape against the metal rod, and I surreptitiously grab a tissue and blot at my wet eyes.

"Friends from college."

"Gotcha. Oh, this one!"

Savannah holds out a red top. Her raised eyebrows seek my approval.

"Perfect," I tell her.

"I'll go get dressed. You better get changed too. Drew's shift starts" —she looks down at her watch— "in ten minutes."

Savannah leaves, and I grab the first dress I see in my closet. As I'm pulling the dress over my head, my phone chirps with a text. I grab it and see Aidan's name.

I miss you.

I stare at those three little words. I miss him too. Terribly. But how can you miss something you only had for such a short time? And how can you miss something that's technically still there? Another text comes through.

I'm a straw.

Immediately I understand what he means. He's empty on the inside.

I write back. **I'm a straw too.**

I wait for those three response dots to appear, but none do. After a minute, I set down the phone and finish getting ready. When Savannah and I are walking to the elevator, my phone chirps again. It's Aidan.

Best?

I'm still here, I write back.

He doesn't say anything else. Perhaps that's all he needed to know.

20

NATALIE

CHARITY AND MARI HAVE MET US AT THE BAR. I'VE NEVER SEEN either of them so done up, but they are both single and this is a bar, so I guess the math makes sense. Drew approaches our table with a third round. In his hands are two martini glasses, Savannah is behind him with the other two.

"Thank you," she coos after the drinks are set on the table. She pulls him in for a kiss, and I look away as the kiss turns deeper. Charity sticks her fingers between her lips and whistles loudly. Savannah laughs and sits down while Drew retreats to his place behind the bar.

Mari lifts her glass into the air. "To Natalie. I hope you get the hell out of the funk you've been in."

"What are you talking about? I haven't been in a funk." I clink my glass against the others and take a sip.

Savannah nods as she swallows. "Yes, you have. I would know." She gives me a pointed look. "I live with you."

There are three sets of eyes staring at me now, and I don't know if it's that or the martinis, but I open my mouth and tell them everything. I need more people to confide in than my sister. She may only be four hours away, but sometimes it feels like so much more.

"The hot guy from the street... Wow. How was it?" Charity leans forward, ready to hear the juicy details. Under the table, Savannah finds my hand and gives it a squeeze. She understands that this goes much, much deeper than sex.

Everything inside me has been so heavy for so long, as though my blood has been replaced by lead. Instead of talking about my broken heart, I tell them something fun and light. I tell them about Aidan's jealousy over the best man, how I found Aidan in the greenhouse and then we decided to get a room. All three of them make different gleeful sounds of surprise when I tell them we ran into Beckett in the hallway.

Charity drinks the last of her martini. "You've left out the part about the steamy sex, but I'll let you slide this time. I wish your story had a happier ending."

I swallow the lump in my throat. "Me too." Apparently happy endings really are just for romance novels and those who get extremely lucky. In my twenty-eight years, I've been very unlucky.

"Why don't you fight for him?" Mari asks.

Of course I've thought about it. It sounds so tragic and romantic, but this isn't a book. We exist in the real world, where choices have consequences. I might win Aidan, but what will I be taking from others?

"I won't do that to Allison."

"But you don't know her. I don't mean to sound unkind, but..."

"Put yourself in Allison's shoes," Savannah says. "You wind up pregnant by a guy you're having casual sex with. If you had feelings for him," Savannah glances at me, then back to Mari, "Wouldn't you want the chance to see where things could go?"

"I can't even imagine being pregnant," Charity says, shuddering. "No thank you."

I'm growing tired of this conversation. We either need to move on to a new topic, or it's time for me to leave. I pick up my martini glass, drink the last of it, and move to set it down. I misjudge the table and end up placing the martini glass on the edge. It teeters for a moment, then falls to the ground and shatters.

"Shit," I mutter.

"Bartender," Charity cups her hands around her mouth and pretends to yell at Drew, "Do not serve this lady any more alcohol."

"Ha ha, very funny," I say, looking down. For the most part, the mess is between my and Savannah's chairs, but there are a few large pieces in the walkway. Steadying myself with one hand on Savannah's chair, I bend at the waist and try to move the glass before it hurts somebody.

Only, it hurts me instead.

"Ow." I sit up in my chair and cradle my right hand in my left. The pain sears my palm. As much as I don't want to look at the cut, I force myself to. Blood oozes from the wound, making it hard to determine how deep it is. All I know is that it really fucking hurts.

Snatching a napkin off the table, I press it to the wound.

Savannah is deep in conversation with Charity and Mari. Something about how choosing to not to have children does not make her less of a woman. Charity gasps when her eyes flicker across the table and spots the red soaking through the napkin.

"I'm all right," I say automatically. Truthfully, I'm not sure I'm okay. I've cut myself before, but it didn't hurt this bad.

Savannah goes to the bar and returns with more napkins. When I pull away the used one, I catch a glimpse of the depth of the cut. It's pretty deep, and my stomach is starting to feel uneasy. Pressing a fresh napkin to my palm, I ask Savannah to put my purse across my body and help me into my jacket.

"Are you going home?" she asks.

"Urgent care," I answer. "I think I might need stitches."

"I'll go with you," she says, standing up from the table.

"We all will."

A loud song has come on, and I'm not sure if it was Mari or Charity who said that, so I shake my head at both of them. "Don't let me ruin your night. I mean it." When I see the looks of disbelief on their faces, I remind them that they did not get dolled up just to go sit in urgent care.

"And I did?" Savannah smiles as she says it, grabbing my jacket and holding it for me while I slip my left arm in. I ball up my right hand, even though it hurts like hell, so that the napkin stays in place, then push my hand through the arm of my jacket.

"Let me go tell Drew what's going on. I'll be back in two seconds." Savannah walks away, weaving her way through the crowd to the bar.

Turning back to Charity and Mari, I apologize for ruining their night.

Mari shakes her head. "The only person whose night is ruined is yours. And you're the one who could probably use a fun night."

"Don't worry about me. I'll be okay." *Try telling that to my heart who won't let me go more than ten minutes without thinking of Aidan.*

"All set?" Savannah asks from behind me.

We say goodbye and make our way through the front door. Savannah holds out her phone and squints at it. "There's an urgent care this way. Come on," she says authoritatively, looping one arm through the crook of my left elbow.

We arrive at urgent care, and Savannah signs me in. The receptionist holds out forms for me to fill out, which clearly I cannot do. Savannah plucks them from her hand and chooses a seat at the far end of the room. According to the monitor in the corner underneath the ceiling, there is approximately a one hour wait time. The chairs are plastic and uncomfortable. A small bookshelf houses toys, puzzles, and books. I bet every one of those items is crawling with nasty germs. On the middle of one wall is a flat screen TV playing *When Harry Met Sally*. I'm not certain, but I think the orgasm scene has passed. Of all that is currently happening in my life, that is something I'm grateful for. I can't imagine sitting in a room full of sick or injured strangers and watching Meg Ryan simulate an orgasm.

Savannah fills in my information as much as she can, asking me questions as she goes. For an hour I try to get comfortable (not possible), and I try not to think of Aidan (also not possible). Is he with her right now? What was the doctor's appointment like? In my imagination, Aidan stands beside Allison as she lies on the exam table, her stomach exposed to the ultrasound technician. The rapid sound of the baby's heartbeat fills the air, and then the tiny little dot of the human appears on the screen. This miracle does something to Aidan, and he looks at Allison with brand-new eyes.

Squeezing my eyes shut, I force myself to get ahold of my imagination. When it comes to writing, my imagination is a gift. In this moment, it's more of a curse.

"Natalie?" My head snaps up. An overweight man in dark brown scrubs stares expectantly at me. His eyes are dull, and when I get closer to him, I see that their color matches his scrubs.

Savannah comes with me. We're led to an exam room where the nurse asks me questions about my injury and takes my temperature, then tells me the doctor will be in shortly. Savannah sits in a chair in the corner, and I'm up on the exam table with the paper that crunches every time I move.

"Sorry," I start to say, but she waves me off.

"Don't be. I'm just sorry you're having to go through this." She nods at my hand. "And about Aidan."

"We'll be okay," I say automatically because I don't know what else to say. Any other ending, any other possibility, is something I cannot fathom.

Doubt swims in Savannah's eyes. "Do you really believe that, Natalie?"

"I have to," I whisper. The truth is, I'll take Aidan any way I can have him. Even if it means he belongs to someone else. He did that for me, and I can do that for him.

My phone rings. Savannah digs it out of my purse and looks at it.

"It's your sister." She holds the phone out to me with raised eyebrows.

"I'll call her back."

Savannah replaces the phone into the side pocket of my

purse. There is a light knock on the door, and then it pushes open. A tall man with a bright, shiny smile steps in. Looking at him is like being at the beach. He has hair the color of sand and eyes the color of the ocean. Nothing like the unhappy nurse.

"Ms. Shay, hello. I'm Dr. Decker." He leans a hip against the small countertop and glances at my hands. "Knife fight?"

I laugh. "You should see the other guy."

He pushes off the counter. It only takes him three steps to cross the small exam room. "Let's take a look," he says. He uses his foot to pull over a stool and sinks down on to it. I peel back the blood spotted napkin and offer him my right hand. He forms a cup with his hands and slips it under my right hand, holding it up and peering closer.

"Ouch," he says, his lips receding to make a face that reminds me of the teeth-baring emoji. "It's good you came in. That's going to need stitches."

I make a face, and he chuckles. "It won't be so bad. I'll give you a little whiskey and some piggin' string to bite on."

"Piggin' string?" I say at the same time that Savannah says, "Are you from Texas? How do you know what piggin' string is?" Her accent gets a little heavier now, just because she has referenced her home state.

"Can somebody please tell me what piggin' string is?" I ask, and they both smile at the joke I'm clearly not in on.

"It's used for calf roping," Dr. Decker explains. "And obviously I'm kidding. I'll use a local anesthetic. You might feel a tugging sensation, but you won't feel pain. Sound good?"

"Sounds a lot better than piggin' string."

Dr. Decker chuckles. "Give me a few minutes to get everything set up, and we'll get started." He turns to Savannah. "Based upon your accent, I guess you are Texas born and bred."

"You bet I am." Pride colors her voice. "And based on your accent, I'd say you are not."

"Nope. I grew up here in the city. I went to UT Austin for my undergrad." His eyes grow soft, nostalgic. A smile lifts one side of his mouth. "I'd like to go back someday. Austin left a mark on me." Gathering my file from the counter, he looks back at me. "I'll be back in a few minutes. Try not to bleed out."

"I'll try," I echo as the door closes softly shut behind him.

"Holy hell, hot doctor alert." Savannah hisses, getting up from her chair and crossing the two feet of space between us. She's so close that I can smell the vodka from the martinis on her breath. I wonder if Dr. Decker smelled that on me too.

"Yeah, he's cute. Too bad you're in a relationship."

"You're not," she points out.

"Don't even try it," I warn. "I want no part of that. It's been less than two weeks since Aidan told me about Allison."

"Is there a statute of limitations on breakups?"

"That doesn't make any sense."

"I know, but it sounded good."

My phone rings again, and Savannah pulls it out from my purse. "Sydney again." She holds it out to me. I take it with my left hand and answer the call.

"Hey, Syd, it's not a super great time to talk right now."

"I'm coming for New Year's!"

Her announcement distracts me from the pain in my right hand. "That's amazing. You can stay with us." I look to

Savannah, and she shrugs and nods. Angling the phone away from my lips, I mouth the words, "*one night.*"

Sydney starts talking about her finals at the same time that Dr. Decker walks back into the room. He slides a tray with various instruments on it onto the counter. "Sydney," I interrupt her mid-sentence. "I have to run. No big deal, but I'm at urgent care. I cut my hand and I'm getting stitches."

"What!" she shrieks. I pull the phone away from my ear. "Don't say any more, you know blood disgusts me." Her words trickle out into the small room.

Dr. Decker smirks. "Me too."

"Sydney, I have to go. The doctor thinks he's funny." I glare jokingly at him. "Bye."

Sydney is saying something else, but I hang up.

Dr. Decker is back on his stool. I hand the phone to Savannah, then look back at him. "Ready."

He slips on gloves and tells me how this will go: disinfect, anesthetize, suture.

All his joking aside, he is a very good doctor. He has steady hands and a good bedside manner. If I ever need stitches again, I'll call him. Assuming he's not back in Austin by then, anyway.

When the procedure is finished, he pushes back from me and removes his gloves. He tosses them in the trash and washes his hands in the sink at the end of the counter. "You were a very good patient."

"Do I get a lollipop?" I ask.

"Of course," he says, laughing. "I don't have any, but you're more than welcome to pick one up on your way home."

I point at Savannah. "Did you hear that? You're in charge of making sure I get a lollipop."

"Actually." Dr. Decker clears his throat. He looks uncertain for the first time since he walked in this exam room tonight. "Do you think I could take you for a lollipop sometime?"

I freeze. My ability to make witty banter has disappeared. "Oh. I, um..."

"Yes," Savannah says, coming to stand beside me. "And guess what Natalie likes even more than lollipops? Gin and tonic." Savannah loops her arm through mine. "I believe you already have her number? She filled out eleventy billion forms when we got here. Correction: I filled them out for her. You have permission to look at them for her number."

Savannah's sly complaint breaks through the awkwardness of the moment.

Dr. Decker opens the door. "Okay then. I guess I'll call you sometime." He flashes that brilliant smile that he first walked in with, and then he's gone from sight. I'm sure there are many other people in need of his attention.

"Savannah," I start, but she lifts her hand to quiet me.

"I know, I know. Not now. But someday, you might want that doctor to call you. And I didn't want you to miss the opportunity."

It's precisely what I'm doing for Aidan. It might tear me up inside, but I want him to have this opportunity.

Knowing this makes me feel the tiniest fraction better. But even the tiniest fraction is not nearly enough to soothe the ache in my chest. I want to call Aidan and tell him what happened tonight, but I'm afraid. What if he is with her?

This is precisely why some people would've told us not to be together. If things were as they were before, and Allison was pregnant, Aidan would still be the person I tell my nothings to. Nothings are what truly bond us to someone else. Nothings are the unimportant moments in a day, the ones you would never think to share with most people. *The cashier at Duane Reade gave me a dirty look. The mean girl from high school sent me a friend request.*

That night in a hotel room, and the two weeks that followed, altered us irrevocably.

I love Savannah, and I love Sydney, but I miss my best friend.

Who will hear my nothings now?

21

AIDAN

ROB WANTS TO PLAY A PICKUP GAME OF BASKETBALL.

I want to continue to lie in bed and mope. My chest feels like a monster with gnarled fingers reached into me and tore out my heart. He took my love *and* my best friend.

Technically, Natalie is still here. Those were almost her exact words. *I'm still here.* But she's not. My Natalie is gone. In her place is someone who is keeping a careful distance from me. I don't blame her. Who wouldn't? We'd barely begun to discover a new side to us when Allison came in and blew us away with her news. From the moment Allison told me, I knew exactly what Natalie would do. With every step I took away from that cafe, I was slowly saying goodbye to what Natalie and I had started.

This feeling in my chest is precisely why I've avoided love. Even in my short time with Natalie, I've learned how high the highs can be. And now I know just how deep the lows can go. It's fucking awful.

"Are you coming?" Rob opens my door for a second time this morning and walks in. He's dressed in basketball shorts with compression pants underneath and a sweatshirt.

"No." I palm my cheek, running my hand down over my chin. My five o'clock shadow is long gone. At this point, I'm almost ready for a camping trip. My face would be well protected by the near-beard on my face.

"What the fuck is eating you?"

"Nothing," I grumble.

"You can lie to your students when you tell them there won't be a pop quiz on Monday," Rob points back at himself, "but you can't lie to me. What gives?"

Obviously Rob doesn't know about Natalie, but he also doesn't know about Allison yet. A small part of me was hoping that if I didn't talk about what was going on, maybe it would just go away. Lying here in my bed with my aching chest, I still don't want to talk about it. I throw back the covers and sit up.

"Get out of here so I can change."

"Are you coming?"

Nodding, I stand up and grab some clothes. Rob backs out and shuts the door.

ALLISON CALLED WHILE I WAS PLAYING BASKETBALL AND WANTS to go crib shopping. I think it seems a little early for that, but what the hell do I know?

Crib shopping it is. I meet Allison outside of a boutique on the Upper East Side. The storefront is fancier than my parents' apartment, which tells me what to expect on the price tags of their items.

"Hi," she says, smiling and kissing my cheek.

Before the ultrasound, Allison was short with me. I walked into the waiting room at the doctor's office and looked around for her. I looked at belly after belly in various stages of growth, and then I spotted Allison's still slim figure. When my eyes met hers, she gave me an icy glare and looked away. The seats on either side of her were taken, so I found a spot a few feet away. When her name was called, she marched ahead of me and didn't acknowledge me until the medical assistant left the exam room.

"Where's Natalie? Did she let you off your leash?" she'd asked me, her arms crossed in front of herself.

I ignored her comment and instead told her that Natalie had chosen to end things with me given the current circumstances. The second the words left my mouth, Allison's mood changed. She has been smiling and warm ever since.

"Are you excited to look at cribs?" She steps back and waits for my answer.

"Yeah, of course." It's what I'm supposed to say.

Allison leads the way into the boutique. For the next hour, I follow her around, looking at everything from cribs to changing tables to onesies that are so small they look like they could fit my foot.

By the time we make it to the register, I'm sweating bullets. Allison has picked up more furniture than what's inside my small room. *You're going to have to open up your trust fund to take care of this baby. Might as well start while it's still in utero.*

One salesgirl rings up what Allison has chosen. A second walks up and stands beside her. She smiles at both of us and asks Allison when she is due.

"August eighth," Allison responds, giddy.

"You must be a planner," salesgirl number one says, glancing up from her computer.

Allison nods. "Yep. Plus, my job keeps me so busy that when I have a free day, I have to take advantage of it."

Salesgirl number one recites the total, and Allison reaches for her wallet. She hands over a credit card without even looking at me. Allison signs the receipt and schedules the furniture delivery for six weeks out.

"You two make such a cute couple. You're going to be great parents." Her smile is wide enough to reveal most of her teeth. Her statement annoys me. How the hell does she know we're going to make great parents? Maybe I'm repulsed by kids. Maybe Allison won't have a motherly bone in her body. *Ugh*. Thank god she can't read my mind.

She hands Allison a white bag containing the smaller items Allison has purchased.

Allison glances up at me, her eyes wary. Despite this, there is a smile on her lips. "Thanks," she says, looking back at the salesgirls.

I have no idea what my face looks like right now. If my face reflects how I'm feeling, then it should be bloodied and bruised, like it's been hit with a hammer. Because that's how I feel on the inside.

We step out onto the sidewalk, and Allison looks up at me, waiting for me to say something. I'm starving, and I'm sure Allison is too, so I ask her if she wants to get something to eat.

"I'm always hungry." She laughs and gently pats her mid-section. "Especially for Italian."

I know of a good place a few blocks away. On our walk there, she curls her arm around mine, her hand gripping my forearm.

She doesn't say anything. Not a damn word. But I can feel something radiating from her. Is it contentment? Happiness?

When our food has been delivered, and my mouth is full of chicken parmesan, Allison tells me she wants to introduce me to her parents.

"Why?" It's a stupid question, but it was the first thing I thought. Other than Natalie, I've never been in a meet-the-parents scenario.

She gives me a look. "Because we are going to raise their grandchild."

"Right. Of course." I sip my water.

"Have you told your parents yet?"

I shake my head. I've been avoiding my mom's phone calls. I not only have to tell her that Natalie and I are not a thing when I know she was assuming we were, but I have to tell her I'm having a baby with Allison.

"I'd like it if you would tell them sooner rather than later. So they can be involved." She looks down at her hands. "I'm assuming they want to be, anyway."

I sit back in my seat and sip from my drink. "Honestly, I haven't thought about it."

Tears fill her eyes. "Are you still in shock? It's been two weeks since I've told you. I thought you'd be... I don't know, *in action* by now. But you're not. You're stagnant. You don't seem excited."

Sighing, I run a hand over my face. How do I explain to her that I'm not excited because I'm fucking heartbroken? I can't say that, because that would break her heart, and breaking a pregnant woman's heart is incredibly far down on the list of things I want to do.

"There are just a lot of thoughts swirling around in my

head," I tell her. *Truth.* "Remember, I wasn't exactly expecting this." *Truth.* "But I'm coming around, I promise." *Lie.*

I'd never imagined what it would be like to see my baby on an ultrasound screen, but if I ever had, what I felt that day wouldn't have been it. The expectant father should feel happy, right? I didn't. But for Allison's sake, I faked it. I smiled at her. She reached for my hand, squeezing it as the technician measured the tiny dot on the screen, and I squeezed her back. She needed me in that moment, and I couldn't deny her that. It's not as if she planned for this either.

A single tear slips down Allison's cheek, but despite this, she attempts a smile. "Coming around is something I can work with." And then she reaches across the table and covers my hand with her own.

I don't know what to say, or what to do, but I do know that right now I should not move my hand. It's like that day at the doctor's office. Allison needs me to be her knight in shining armor. She needs me to step up and be the person she imagined having a baby with.

For the first time in my life, I have a broken heart.

For the millionth time in my life, I'm going to have to lie about love.

22

NATALIE

THE WHEELS ON SYDNEY'S SMALL SUITCASE ROLL TO A STOP IN the middle of our apartment. She came in on the four o'clock train, and after a stop for a black and white cookie at her favorite place, we made it back to my place. She turns in a circle, her arms outstretched. "This place is amazing. Way better than that shithole you shared with Henry."

My old apartment wasn't a shithole. The opposite, actually. Unless she's using the apartment as a metaphor for our marriage, but even then she'd be wrong. We failed because we were wrong for each other, plain and simple.

"Sydney, this is Savannah." I indicate my hand toward the kitchen where Savannah stands. She's just cut an apple, and waves with the hand holding the knife. "Sorry," she laughs, setting it down and waving a second time, this time knife-free.

It's New Year's Eve, a day that holds no excitement for me. I'd rather stay in and watch a movie until my eyes close, preferably by ten p.m. With Sydney in town, I know that won't be happening.

"Hi," Sydney says, walking to the kitchen and leaning on the counter. "Are you ready to ring in the New Year?"

Savannah starts talking about our plans for the night, and I take Sydney's bag into my room and push it against the wall. When I come back out, Savannah is still talking.

"We've been together for forever, but neither of us feel the need to make the next big step. Society has determined we should be married with two kids by now, but" —she shakes her head, her long blonde hair swishing— "no thank you. We're doing things our way."

Sydney claps. Her inner feminist is doing backflips. "Bravo. Good for you."

Savannah bows and nearly hits her forehead on the sink. She straightens, cringing at the nearness.

"No more accidents," I tell her. "One trip to urgent care in the past week was enough." As if she needs the reminder.

"Ahh, but if Dr. Sexy is there, the trip might be worth it," Savannah counters, one finger lifted in the air.

"Dr. Sexy?" Sydney reaches over and swipes a slice of apple from Savannah's plate. "Do tell."

I shake my head. "There's nothing to tell."

Savannah gives me a look. "Except that there is."

"Out with it," Sydney says around a mouthful of apple.

I resist the urge to roll my eyes. "The doctor who stitched me up was cute. End of story."

"*Not* the end of story," Savannah states. She looks at Sydney. "He asked for her number."

Sydney's eyes widen. "Did you give it to him?"

"Savannah made sure he got it." I open the fridge and peer into it. I'm not hungry, but I want something to do with my hands while I'm being interrogated.

"You bet I did," she says proudly.

"Doesn't matter." I close the fridge and walk away. "I don't want to see him."

"At some point, you will," Savannah insists.

And what point will that be? When Aidan tells me the gender of his baby? Or when I receive the begrudgingly sent invitation for Allison's baby shower? Those things loom in the distance like dark clouds dancing over the horizon. I wish I could shut my eyes and turn my back on them.

I realize that I can't. I can't quit life. I can't quit showing up for my friends and family. Even when that means showing up for Aidan with a smile on my face, even when my heart is crying.

"Hey," Savannah says, leaving the kitchen and coming to my side. She places an arm over my shoulders and pulls me in tight. "It's going to be okay. We're going to go out tonight. You're going to put on something hot. You're going to ring in the New Year like it's your job. This next year is going to be your best. Trust me."

I do as Savannah says because it's so much easier. I wear a red dress with a low-cut neckline. I drink champagne, and at midnight, I kiss my sister's cheek. Aidan calls a few minutes after. I duck out of the bar to get away from all the noise. The street isn't that much better, but at least I'm away from the cacophony of voices.

"Happy New Year." His deep voice is low and gravelly, wrapping around my champagne soaked thoughts and sneaking into my heart.

"Happy New Year," I echo, the words slipping slowly from my throat.

He chuckles. "Have you been enjoying the champagne?"

I giggle. "Veuve."

"The good stuff."

"Savannah's boyfriend was being generous."

"I see."

"Did you have fun tonight?" As wrong as it is, I hope the answer is no.

"I didn't go anywhere if that's what you're asking."

"Did you have people over?" Let's be honest, that's not what I'm actually asking.

His low laughter rumbles through the phone. "Allison wasn't here."

"Am I that transparent?"

"No. I just know you that well."

Cradling the phone between my ear and my shoulder, I cross my arms in front of myself and try to warm up as much as I can. In my haste to answer Aidan's call, I left my jacket inside.

"Natalie, I'm not sure what to say."

"Me either," I respond, my voice low.

"How about we go see one of those old movies I hate? What's playing?"

Closing my eyes, I tip my chin up to the sky. Relief trickles down through me at Aidan's invitation of doing something so normal. "I'll check and let you know."

"If you don't call me in two days, I'm going to call you back."

I smile. "You better."

"Bye, Natalie."

"Bye, Aidan."

I look down at my phone and watch it darken. I might be standing out here in the freezing cold, but I'm happier than I've been all night. With a stupid grin on my face, I turn and head back to the front door of the bar. And right into the shoulder of a tall guy in a black pea coat.

"Sorry," I mumble, staggering back a couple feet. I regain my footing and look up to see who I attempted to mow down. The guys face is nearly slack, as if his facial muscles have given up for the night. He looks at me through slitted eyes, and a loose, lazy smile pulls up one side of his mouth.

"Well, hello there," he says, taking a step toward me.

Automatically I back up, and at the same time two of the people he is with grab onto each of his shoulders.

"Sorry, he's drunk," one of his buddies explains, as if it's not obvious.

My eyes widen when I see who is holding onto the drunk guy's right shoulder.

"Dr. Decker?"

He squints. "Lollipop?"

"That's not my name."

He laughs. "I know that, Natalie. Lollipop is how I've been referring to you in my head."

I stiffen. That means he has been thinking about me. I haven't thought of him at all, not until Savannah brought him up earlier today.

Dr. Decker's friend sways, causing the men on either side of him to sway also. "Whoa, Brad."

"Whoa yourself, Dr. Decker," Brad says, snickering.

Ignoring his friend, Dr. Decker looks at me and says, "We should probably get him home." Brad starts walking away, taking the two guys with him. Dr. Decker looks back at me and I wave.

"Grady," he says.

"What?" I must've heard him wrong.

"My name," he shouts. He's two storefronts away now. "It's Grady."

The crowd on the sidewalk swallows him, and soon all I

can see are three heads bobbing farther and farther from me.

"Bizarre," I murmur and go back into the bar. I find Savannah and Sydney and tell them what happened.

"It's a sign," Sydney says drunkenly.

"A sign of what?" I ask.

"I don't know," she mutters, laying her head down on my shoulder.

Savannah says goodbye to Drew, and the three of us head back home. When Sydney is lying in bed beside me snoring, I pull out my phone and bring up the picture Aidan used for my online dating profile.

I stare at it and pray we can make it through this.

23

AIDAN

Natalie and I have seen four movies in four weeks. Allison is fifteen weeks pregnant and has begun to show. I still haven't told my mother.

But I'm about to. She and my dad asked me to get lunch with them and considering this week Allison and I have an appointment to learn the gender of the baby, I guess it's time. Allison asked if she could come today, but I told her it would be best if I told them alone. I don't know what they'll say, and I don't want her present for that. They can meet her another time.

Allison wants to be a family. In some ways, she is a lot like Natalie. She wants things to be the way the world thinks they should be. I know she wants that, but am I supposed to give it to her? I keep waiting. I take her out for dinner, for walks, to get green smoothies. I'm stepping into the role of expectant parent like I'm supposed to, but I'm still waiting for *it* to happen. To feel something for her. To feel connected to the life growing inside her.

Maybe the reason *it* isn't happening is because I can't get Natalie out of my head. When I'm not with her, which is often, I'm thinking of her. Her smile, her sense of humor, her playfulness. Last week I saw a homeless man fall in the street, and immediately I thought of how Natalie would've hurried to help him. I was across the street and couldn't get there in time, and by the time the cars passed, and I could see him again, people had already come to his aid. Natalie would've teared up over that, and I would've pulled her close and kissed away her sadness.

When I arrive at the restaurant, I learn my parents are already seated. They both stand up when they see me coming and hug me when I reach the table.

My mom sits down and rubs her hands together, her eyes gleaming. "I have some good news for you. Well, Natalie really. I just came from my editor's office." Her shoulders shake with her excitement. "My editor loves her book. She wants to meet with Natalie."

I beam, wishing badly that Natalie were here so I could watch her digest this news. "She'll be thrilled." I always knew her dreams were going to come true. For a person as good and kind as Natalie, the universe had to come through for her. It just had to.

"You should've brought her to lunch today," Dad says, taking a sip of his wine and setting it back down on the white linen tablecloth.

The waiter stops by our table and I order an iced tea. Pulling my hands together on the tabletop, I lean forward, glancing back and forth between my parents. "There's something I have to tell you."

Mom's eyes get big. "Is Natalie pregnant?" She slaps a hand over mouth, and a muffled '*sorry*' slips out.

I shake my head. "No, but Allison is." *Boom. Bomb dropped.*

My parents both wear a look as if someone has told them aliens will be joining us for lunch.

"Who is Allison?" my dad asks.

"A woman I was seeing before Natalie. It was very casual." I remove my hands from the table and wipe my palms on my jeans. It's not easy trying to find the nicest way to explain to my parents that Allison was somebody I met just for sex.

I sit back, giving my parents some time to absorb the news. Dad takes a big gulp of his chardonnay. Mom captures her lower lip between two fingers and twists.

Releasing her lip, she says, "You've really managed to fuck this up."

"I know."

"Where does Natalie fit into this?"

Staring at the iced tea the server placed in front of me, I say, "Natalie and I are still friends."

I look up into my mother's knowing eyes.

"No more than that?" she asks.

"Natalie reacted the way I knew she would. She bowed out."

"She wanted to give you the chance to explore this situation with Allison. She didn't want to be in the way." Dad places his hand over my mother's. "I know someone else who is like that."

Mom uses her free hand to pass over the top of Dad's hand. "Anyone who has ever said that love should only feel good, is a fool."

It's a famous line from the book she wrote about herself and my father's relationship. It's been printed on T-shirts and mugs. Readers have tattooed it on themselves and then mailed their pictures to my mother.

I push around ice cubes with my straw. "I understand that. But does it have to feel so damn awful?"

"It can only feel really bad if at first it was really good."

"Which book is that from?"

My mom taps her head with a finger. "That was from up here." She moves her hand over her heart. "And here."

For the rest of lunch, I tell them more about Allison. We talk about how far along she is, and by the end, my parents are hesitant but in the beginning phase of excitement. I promise to call them as soon as I know the gender. They would like to meet her, so I promise to make plans for that also.

We part ways, and I know my mother is on her way home to call Natalie. It's the first sliver of happiness I've felt since I saw Allison standing across the street from school on that snowy day. I only wish I was sharing in the happy news with her.

After what happened with Henry, and then me, Natalie deserves a win.

24

NATALIE

I'M IN THE MIDDLE OF A COMPLICATED BRAID WHEN MY PHONE rings. I lean over, glance at the screen, and drop my hair.

"Diana, hi. How are you?" I brush aside the hair that has slipped out of the plait and into my eyes.

"Natalie! It's good to hear your voice. I've missed you."

The apologetic tone of her voice tells me she knows about me and Aidan.

"I've missed you too."

"I have to be honest, I didn't just call because I missed you. I have some good news for you."

Thank fuck. I could use some.

"My editor loved your book. She wants to meet with you."

I let out a noise, a cross between a squeal and what I imagine an otter sounds like. Diana laughs. "I told you the news was good."

"That's the best news I've had in a while." My nose starts to burn and I'm struggling to keep the happy tears at bay.

"So I've heard."

"You have?"

"Aidan told us today, at lunch. How are you?"

"Not great," I admit.

"I'm sorry, Natalie. This wasn't the way things were supposed to go."

The tears that were happy quickly turn sad. "I thought Aidan and I were going to sail off into the sunset."

"You know what you can do now? You can write your own happy ending. Literally. You can turn this into a book. Friends-to-lovers. Something along those lines."

I sniff. "Look at that, I already have an idea for book two. Provided by none other than the First Lady of romance." I turn serious. "Thank you, Diana. For giving me a chance."

"I got you in the door, but your work stood on its own two feet. Don't discount that."

"Yes, ma'am."

She chuckles. "Will you come and see me sometime soon?"

"Of course."

"Keep your head up, okay sweetie? Everything will work out. I have a good feeling."

We hang up and I squeal a second time, only this time it's much louder than before. Then I pick up the phone and call Sydney. When she doesn't answer, I leave her a rambling voicemail. Just as I am about to set down the phone, a text message from an unknown number comes through.

Hi, Natalie. This is Grady. Or Dr. Decker, as you called me on New Year's Eve. Would you be interested in a gin and tonic sometime?

Maybe it's my giddiness over the book.

Maybe it's the fact that I'm so fucking sick of hurting.

I respond and accept his offer.

* * *

THE BAR WHERE I'VE AGREED TO MEET GRADY IS ONLY A FEW blocks from my place. It's old school, with the booths tucked away in corners, and dark lighting. Grady waves when I walk in. His hair is freshly cut and neatly combed. He wears a light blue sweater over a white collared shirt. He is handsome and a doctor, making him every mother's dream for her daughter.

The closer I get to his table, the more I realize that his hair annoys me. It's too perfect. I want to run my hands through it and mess it up. Is the rest of Grady just as boring as his hair? Maybe not. He had a good bedside manner when he was stitching me up. He was funny. Perhaps these traits can make up for his humdrum hair.

Shedding my jacket, I placed it on the back of the chair and sink down. Grady signals for the server, and when she comes over he orders a gin and tonic for me.

"Is that alright?" he asks, his eyebrows forming a 'V.' "Would you prefer something different? I can call her back over here."

I wave him off. "No, that's perfect. Thank you."

Grady smiles at me. He leans back and crosses one ankle over the opposite knee. "So, who did you kiss on New Year's Eve?"

His question takes me by surprise. "Excuse me?"

"The last time I saw you, it was right after the clock struck midnight. It wasn't until I got home that night that I thought about who was lucky enough to have your lips on theirs."

I shake my head. "Nobody. Unless you count my sister."

Grady blinks twice. "You kissed your sister?"

"On the cheek," I clarify.

Grady narrows his eyes. "You didn't kiss a fella?"

I laugh at the word *fella*. "I didn't kiss a fella. Or bite any piggin' string. Did you kiss a dame?"

He nods. "Of course. How else do you ring in the New Year?"

"Did you know her? Or was she a stranger?" The server sets my drink down in front of me and walks away.

"Stranger," Grady says nonchalantly.

"You kissed a stranger?" I ask, incredulous.

"Isn't that what New Year's Eve is all about?" He grins. "Scratch that. I know that's not what it's all about. Besides, she kissed me more than I kissed her. Anyway, let's move on to a different topic. What did you do today?"

I sip my drink and tell him, "I went to the Social Security office and filed for a name change."

He pauses mid-reach for his drink. "I wasn't expecting you to say that."

I chuckle. "I'm changing my last name back to Maxwell."

Grady has regained his composure and now has his beer firmly in his grip. "Back to?"

"My divorce was final a few months ago."

"You hardly look old enough to be divorced. You hardly look old enough to have been married."

Maybe I should just tell him that I'm still suffering from a broken heart from another man, and then I can watch him sprint out of here.

I smile at the thought and tell him I'm gathering fodder for my future novels.

He asks me about writing, and I share with him my most

recent good news. "I called the editor yesterday. Her secretary set me up for a meeting in two weeks."

He grins and shakes his head. "I can't believe I know somebody famous."

I wag my finger at him. "Not yet."

"You will be. I believe in you."

My smile falters. Aidan has said that exact same thing to me, countless times.

Our date lasts another forty-five minutes. Grady talks about growing up in New York City, and like many other times in my life, I feel grateful my parents raised me in the suburbs. When Grady asks about my parents, I give him basic information. The less detail about them, the better.

Grady walks me out of the bar, and I thank him for the drink. We stand there, locked in that awkward moment at the end of the date. He leans in like he's going to kiss me, and I freeze. At the last moment, I turn my head and his lips land on my cheek.

He pulls back, an embarrassed smile dusting his lips. "I'll see you again soon?" His tone is hopeful.

"Sure," I answer before turning to walk away. I'm going in the wrong direction of my apartment, but I don't care. I just have to get away.

Unwilling to risk a second awkward run-in with Grady, I take a circuitous route home.

When I get home, I find Savannah sitting on the couch thumbing through a magazine. "How'd it go?" she asks, tossing the magazine down beside her. Her eyes, which at first were hopeful, absorb my expression. Their glimmer dulls as she waits for my response.

Holding up a hand, I begin to tick off Grady's attributes that are immediately recognizable. "He's nice. Charming.

Sweet. Funny." I groan. "And a doctor. A freaking doctor, Savannah."

"But?"

I plop down on the couch beside Savannah and pick up her copy of Us Weekly. "He's not Aidan."

25

AIDAN

I'VE TAKEN THE AFTERNOON OFF TO GO WITH ALLISON TO THE big appointment. The gender appointment. She asked me if we should wait to learn, telling me about something she heard of where the doctor's office tells a bakery the gender, and they bake a cake with either blue or pink dye. The expectant parents cut into the cake and that's how they learn what they're having. I'm sure for some people that sounds like a great idea, but it doesn't work for me. When I told her I'd rather just find out the old-fashioned way, she agreed, even though I could see her disappointment.

To make up for my lack of enthusiasm about revealing the gender, I left work early and am going to swing by her apartment and take her to the appointment. Our plan had been to meet there, but this way I can give her some sort of surprise, even if it doesn't have to do with our baby's gender.

I walk up to her building and catch the door just as somebody is walking out. Mumbling my thanks, I hurry inside out of the cold.

I take the elevator to the fourth floor and step off. As

soon as I step foot in the hallway, I hear them: angry voices floating down from somewhere. As I get closer, I see Allison's front door is cracked open. Voices float through the small fissure. A man's, followed by a woman's.

Stepping closer, I push an ear up to the space. My breath quiets as I listen.

"Don't lie to me. I saw the picture on your fridge." I can hear the stress in the man's voice.

"I'm not lying, Jared. It's not yours," Allison insists in a high-pitched voice.

My hand is poised to push open the door, but Jared's next words stop me. "The timing fits, Allison."

What. The. Fuck.

"It's not yours," Allison insists. The pitch in her voice is higher now, desperation leaking through.

"I don't know who you think that baby belongs to, but whoever he is didn't spend a weekend fucking you. And I don't think you need to be reminded that we ran out of condoms halfway through."

"Shut up," Allison screeches. "Just shut up."

"I'm giving you twenty-four hours to tell whoever he is the truth. If you don't, I'll find him myself and tell him."

Footsteps come closer. I step away and hurry down the hall, turning my back toward Allison's place and pretend to be waiting in front of someone else's door. Behind me, I hear Allison's door close and those same footsteps stomp down the hallway to the elevator. A moment later the elevator announces its arrival with a ding. I wait a few more seconds, then turn around. Jared is gone.

Slowly I walk to Allison's door and knock.

She answers with her face already arranged in an

expression of anger. The anger vanishes, and shock takes its place.

"Aidan? What are you doing here?"

"Is that really the question you want to ask, Allison? Don't you mean to ask me if I heard you and Jared?"

She takes a step back, her hand coming up to cover her open mouth. "Aidan, I..." She shakes her head. "I..."

"Why, Allison? Why?"

Tears pour down her face. "I'm sorry. So sorry. Jared... he's my ex. He's not very nice, Aidan. I don't know if he's the father, or you are. I swear on everything, that's the truth. But I do know who I'd rather it be." She looks at me so pitifully, so sorrowfully, but it doesn't displace any of my outrage.

"So you were just going to let me believe I was the father when you didn't know for certain?" *Un-fucking-believable.* I'm such an idiot. I should've pushed for a paternity test the second the words left her lips that day in the cafe.

She nods, shame coloring her cheeks. "I know how awful that sounds, but I just wanted to pretend that the father wasn't somebody like Jared. If he is..." A shudder moves her shoulders. "I don't know if I can handle it. Haven't you ever wished something weren't true?"

"Of course I have. But that doesn't give you the right to mislead me. Not only that but, Natalie. *Natalie.*" I rub my face with my hands. It's hard to say at what point I realize I'm standing in the wrong place. I know I shouldn't be here anymore, and it's like bricks raining down upon me.

"How soon can you get a test?" I ask, my voice intense.

"I'll ask the doctor today," she says tearfully. "It's just a simple blood test and—"

"That's enough," I tell her, backing out of her apartment. She follows, her arm outstretched. "Aidan, I—"

"Bye, Allison."

I hurry to the elevator. As I wait for it, I look back. Allison stands in her doorway, one hand on her stomach and her eyes squeezed shut.

The doors open and I step on, willing the damn thing to go faster. Glancing at my watch, I see it's only mid-afternoon. That means Natalie is still at work. I have an idea, and I hope to hell she comes straight home after work today. But if she doesn't, it doesn't matter. I'll wait all night for her.

I'VE DONE IT. I'VE BEEN UPTOWN, DOWNTOWN, AND everywhere in between. My arms are loaded with Natalie's favorite flower, ice cream, dinner, drink, salsa, and perfume. My final stop is at a store that sells random junk. I came in here once to buy a bottle of water and noticed a basket of heart shaped rocks on the check-out counter.

I push aside the rocks until I find the best one.

"I'll take it," I say, handing it to the lady behind the counter.

She tells me it's one dollar, and I laugh. Such an inexpensive symbol for something so priceless.

I pay her and slip it into one of my bags. I have fifteen minutes until Natalie gets home.

Natalie's building is four blocks away, and I jog the entire distance. Two old women watch in amazement as I go by, but for the most part, nobody notices me. Such is life in a bustling city.

When I get to Natalie's door, I set everything up. Then I sit down, lean my head against the wall and wait. One minute passes, then two, and then after a while, it's twenty. I grab my phone to look at the time, ignoring the urge to text Natalie. My plan is to surprise her, and my text message might tip her off.

Fifteen more minutes go by, and although I've been waiting for it, the ding of the elevator startles me.

Please be Natalie.

It's not. A man in scrubs steps off. He's talking to somebody else, but I can't see who because of the way his body is angled. I hear the response, and I would know that voice anywhere.

I get to my feet just as Natalie's eyes meet mine. She walks toward me, confusion in her eyes.

"Aidan?"

The man in scrubs is still walking beside her, so I stay quiet and wait for him to break off and go into his own apartment. Natalie reaches me, and the guy in scrubs stops alongside her. Instead of looking at me, he's looking at the array of items at our feet.

What the hell is going on?

I point to the guy and look at Natalie, the question plain on my face.

"Aidan, this is Grady. He's the doctor who stitched me up."

Natalie told me about her trip to urgent care, but she didn't tell me she and the doctor had.... had... I can't even finish the sentence. The thought makes me ill.

"What's all this?" she asks, looking down at the ground.

"Just some stuff," I mumble, feeling like an idiot.

Her expression softens. She knows that it's not just *stuff*.

"Natalie, I'm going to take off," Grady says, turning to look at Natalie.

"But what about—"

"Don't worry about it. I'll call Brad."

Grady doesn't touch her. He doesn't run a hand along her arm, hug her goodbye, and thank fuck he doesn't kiss her in front of me. He retreats to the elevator and steps on when it arrives.

"He's locked out of his apartment," Natalie explains, her face guilty. "He needed a place to hang out while he waited for the building manager to let him in."

I nod and stick my hands in my pocket. Now that I'm here, my tongue feels twisted up.

Natalie glances at the ground. "Why are my favorite things on the ground outside my apartment?"

"Because I didn't know what else to do. I wanted to do something grand and amazing for you, but I don't know what that looks like. I'm not good at this, Natalie."

She watches me. I've memorized her face, and now I'm watching her absorb my words, trying to make sense of what is happening.

"Come inside," she tells me, pulling her keys from her purse and opening the door.

I pick everything up and put it back in the bags, except for the heart-shaped rock, which I stow in my pocket. I walk in behind Natalie and set the bag down on the table beside her purse. She hangs her coat on the rack and kicks off her shoes.

Sighing deeply, she turns to where I stand just a few feet inside the door. It's almost the exact spot I stood in when I told her Allison was expecting.

"Okay. Please explain to me what is going on. I'm so confused."

For the past hour, I've had time to plan what to say, but

right now in this moment all I manage to do is blurt out, "The baby might not be mine."

Natalie gasps. Her fingers sail up to touch her parted lips. "Might not?"

I shake my head. "We're getting a blood test to confirm."

"I...I thought it wasn't even a question."

"Me neither," I tell her. The amount of relief I feel overwhelms me, and on my face, I feel a grin that stretches from ear to ear. "We were supposed to find out the baby's gender today, so I went to her apartment to take her to the appointment. She didn't know I was coming, and I overheard her talking with her ex. I'm almost positive he's the father, Natalie. I would bet my life on it."

"But you're not definite?" Hope dances in her eyes, but I can see her trying to quell it.

Every time we've gone to the movies in the past month, I sat beside her while I was dying to reach over and touch her. Now we are having this conversation, separated by a few feet, and I'm done with it.

Striding forward, I make it so we are separated by mere inches. Gripping her shoulders, I look into the eyes of the girl who stole my heart back when I didn't know I had one. "It's true that I don't know what exactly is going to happen. But I do know that no matter what that test says, you're my forever. You think you're doing what's best for me by backing out, but you're not. I've learned that the hard way."

"What if you are the father?"

"Then we'll deal with it. Together. Our situation might not look pretty from the outside, but it will be ours. I don't want to be without you, Natalie." Reaching into my pocket, I pull out the rock and hold it up between us. "You stole my heart when we were seventeen, but I never acted on it. Then that night when you were in the bathtub, you asked me that question. We had so many rules surrounding our friendship, but you broke one that night. And then I realized we were only as strong as the breaking of one rule. Not because we were weak, Natalie, but because we'd been denying ourselves for so long."

I continue. "I'm not perfect, you know that. My parents are unconventional, to say the least. I share an apartment with two guys, and I'm not a doctor."

"I don't need you to be a doctor," Natalie says tearfully. "I love your parents the way they are, and as much as I like Rob and Aaron, I hope that one day soon you won't live with them." She takes the rock from my hand. "I don't need pretty, or perfect. I just need you."

My body crashes against hers, my lips consume her. I touch her, I taste her. She is sunlight in the morning, a drop of dew sliding down a flower petal, a swath of moonlight late at night.

She is everything.

* * *

I'VE BROUGHT NATALIE TO MY PARENTS POUND RIDGE HOUSE for the weekend. We needed a place to escape to, a place where we can be alone, and just be us. No roommates interrupting us. No barking dogs, honking cabs, or previously made plans to get in our way.

We've been here less than seven hours and we've already made good use of the kitchen counter, the laundry room, and the big, fancy dining room table.

"Let's never leave here," Natalie murmurs, her face snuggled into my chest. We're lying on the couch, watching the snow fall outside. Three more inches is expected by the end of the weekend. I'm hoping the forecaster is wrong and we'll get ten more. Snowed in with Natalie sounds like exactly where I want to be.

"Sounds good to me." I place a kiss on the top of her hair. She lifts her head so she can see me.

"I love you, Aidan."

"I love you too, Nat."

She wiggles against me, then glances down and laughs at the reaction she has gotten from me.

"Let me get a drink first. I swear you're working me over-time." She climbs off me and stretches. Reaching down, she snatches the blanket off me and wraps it around herself.

"Hey," I complain. She laughs and walks from the room. While she's gone, I get up and grab a blanket from the woven basket in the corner of the room. I sit back down and wait for Natalie to come back.

A few minutes later she returns, but her demeanor has changed.

"What?" I ask. Whatever it is, we'll tackle it together.

She holds out my phone. "I was getting a drink and heard your phone. Allison sent you a message."

Suddenly time suspends. The snow falls slower so that I can see the individual snowflakes tumbling to the ground. My heartbeats feel more spaced out. I haven't heard from Allison since the day we went for the blood draw. Jared was late, which was fine by me. I gave my blood and got the hell out of there.

"What does it say?" I choke out.

Tears tumble from Natalie's eyes.

I should get up, take the phone from her, read the results for myself, but I can't bring myself to.

Squeezing my eyes shut, I take a deep breath and count to ten. Each second passes, more excruciating than the next. My eyes open.

Natalie comes closer, blanket rustling, and holds out the phone until it's under my nose.

I read the results and find I'm not the only one crying.

EPILOGUE

"I'm just not sure who's going to eat these cupcakes." I sigh theatrically, dipping a finger into the chocolate frosting of one cupcake and bringing it to my mouth.

"Me! I will eat them all!" Brayden screeches, his little voice bouncing off the walls of our kitchen.

"Not all of them," I tell him, wiping my finger on a dish-towel and lightly poking the tip of his nose. "Your mother wouldn't appreciate that."

Allison will be here in half an hour to pick up Brayden. That's just enough time for me to fill the three-year-old with lots of sugar and then hand him off to his mother.

"Did you have fun with us today?" I ask Brayden as I place a cupcake onto a plate and slide it across the counter to where he sits.

He nods and peels off the wrapper. Chocolate crumbs fall down his front when he takes a bite.

Aidan walks in from the living room, his expression hopeful. "Please tell me they're cool enough to eat now."

"Yes, yes," I say, meeting him just as he rounds the

kitchen island. "I'll take her." I reach for the tiny wrapped bundle sleeping in his arms. Juliana is only four weeks old. I'm exhausted, but I've never been happier. She and Aidan fill me with joy on a daily basis.

Aidan grabs a cupcake from the cooling rack and sits down beside Brayden. I stand on the opposite side of the island, watching them. They look so much alike, a stranger would never know they aren't related.

We'd called Allison that day after she sent the test results. Joy was my first reaction, but I couldn't truly feel it when Allison was so devastated.

Two months later Aidan told me he felt bad about her situation and wondered how she was handling everything. I encouraged him to reach out, and he did. We learned that Jared, despite his insistence that day in Allison's apartment, was not actually interested in being a father. He signed away his legal rights to Brayden, and Allison became a single mother.

Unbelievably, Allison and I became friends. Not the ride-or-die kind, but the kind that can have a conversation and walk away feeling better about life. And then later on, when I found out I was pregnant with Juliana, Allison became the person I went to with questions about my changing, aching body. Her son, Brayden, visits us a couple times a month so Allison can get a break. Today, that break included a second date with Grady.

I ran into him when I was eight months pregnant and waddling down Fifth Avenue. I've never thought of myself as a matchmaker, but when I saw him, I immediately thought of her.

For a person who had been so anti-love, Aidan is awfully good at it. He's tender, caring, and knows exactly how to make me laugh. Diana and Diego have taken to the role of grandparents, and Shawn has too. Their love is still a secret, but I don't know for how much longer. Diana says the older she gets, the less she cares about keeping it. As for my book, it was published a year after I first met with the editor. It wasn't a chart-topper, but it sold well. I received an advance for my sophomore effort, and it went to my editor just a few days before Juliana's arrival.

The knock on the door signals Allison's arrival. Brayden squeals and hops off his seat.

"Mommy!" he yells when Aidan opens the door.

Allison walks in and gathers the small, dark-haired human bowling ball into her arms. "Hey, buddy." She glances over at me. "Let's be quiet. Juliana is sleeping."

"That's all she ever does," Brayden complains. The three of us laugh. Aidan picks up Brayden and swings him into the air. "Want to pack a cupcake to go home with you?" They walk away together.

"How was it?" I ask Allison. She peeks at Juliana and makes that face that I've come to expect from people, the one that is filled with reverence.

Allison smiles shyly. "Good. Really good, actually. He wants to meet Brayden. I told him next time."

I grin. "So there will be a next time?"

She nods, her eyes excited. "Definitely."

Aidan comes back in the room with a plastic container and hands it to Allison. She gathers Brayden's jacket and sticks his shoes on his feet. Poking him on the nose, she asks, "Ready to go, little man?"

Brayden leaps up and bounces on an invisible pogo stick to the door.

I walk her to the door and open it. "If things go well with Grady, maybe you can bring him to our wedding."

"Yeah, maybe." She smiles again and takes Brayden's hand.

We wave goodbye and the door closes.

Aidan comes up behind me and wraps his arms around my middle. He settles his chin on my shoulder and quietly asks, "Did you just invite your ex to our wedding?"

I scoff. "He hardly counts as my ex. Did your ex just leave here with a love child she tried to pass off as yours?"

"You win," Aidan says, dropping a kiss on my cheek. "Speaking of love child..." He gazes down at Juliana. "She's going to be up any second demanding dinner."

A few minutes later, Aidan's statement comes true. I settle into a recliner to feed her, and Aidan goes to clean up the mess Brayden and I made in the kitchen.

A baby before a wedding was not what I had for my life plan. Neither was divorcing my college sweetheart or falling in love with my best friend.

Sometimes, the very best in life is what's taking place in the background while we are busy focusing on what we think is right for us.

The End

* * *

VISIT JENNIFER AT JENNIFERMILLIKINWRITES.COM TO JOIN HER mailing list and receive a free novella. She is @jenmillwrites on all social platforms and would love to connect.

ALSO BY JENNIFER MILLIKIN

Hayden Family Series

The Patriot

The Maverick

The Outlaw

The Calamity

Standalone

Here For The Cake

Better Than Most

The Least Amount Of Awful

Return To You

One Good Thing

Beyond The Pale

Good On Paper

The Day He Went Away

Full of Fire

The Time Series

Our Finest Hour - now optioned for Film/TV

Magic Minutes

The Lifetime of A Second

Visit Jennifer at jennifermillikinwrites.com to join her mailing list
and receive a free novella. She is @jenmillwrites on all social

platforms and would love to connect.

ACKNOWLEDGMENTS

Readers- THANK YOU! Thank you for reading, for loving, for spending your time on my work. Thank you for telling your friends, leaving reviews, connecting with me on social media. I love the messages, the posts, the emails. They make all the blood, sweat, and tears of writing a novel worth it.

Ellie McLove, at My Brother's Editor. Thank you for handling this book with care and love.

Sarah Hansen at Okay Creations. Thank you for making this amazing cover. It's stunning.

Julia. My number one beta reader. Your willingness to sling the truth at me makes me better, and it's something I treasure.

ABOUT THE AUTHOR

Jennifer Millikin is a bestselling author of contemporary romance and women's fiction. She is the two-time recipient of the Readers Favorite Gold Star Award, and readers have called her work "emotionally riveting" and "unputdown-able". Following a viral TikTok video with over fourteen million views, Jennifer's third novel, *Our Finest Hour,* has been optioned for TV/Film. She lives in the Arizona desert with her husband, children, and Liberty, her Labrador retriever. With fifteen novels published so far, she plans to continue her passion for storytelling.

facebook.com/JenniferMillikinwrites

instagram.com/jenmillwrites

bookbub.com/profile/jennifer-millikin

Made in the USA
Las Vegas, NV
17 September 2024

95392564R00152